The Monkeys and the Mango Tree

The Monkeys and the Mango Tree

*Teaching Stories of the
Saints and Sadhus of India*

Harish Johari

Illustrations by Pieter Weltevrede

Inner Traditions
Rochester, Vermont

Inner Traditions International
One Park Street
Rochester, Vermont 05767
www.gotoit.com

Library of Congress Cataloging-in-Publication Data
Johari, Harish, 1934–
     The monkeys and the mango tree : teaching stories of the saints and sadhus of India / Harish Johari ; illustrations by Pieter Weltevrede.
          p.   cm.
     ISBN 0-89281-564-7 (pbk. : alk. paper)
     1. Tales—India.   2. Legends—India.   3. Mythology, Indic.
4. Philosophy, Indic.   5. India—Religious life and customs.   I.
Title.
GR305.J56   1998
398.2'0954—dc21   97-38921

Printed and bound in Canada

10 9 8 7 6 5 4 3 2 1

Distributed to the book trade in Canada by Publishers Group
     West (PGW), Toronto, Ontario
Distributed to the book trade in the United Kingdom by Deep
     Books, London
Distributed to the book trade in Australia by Millennium Books,
     Newtown, N.S.W.
Distributed to the book trade in New Zealand by Tandem Press,
     Auckland
Distributed to the book trade in South Africa by Alternative
     Books, Ferndale

꧁꧂

Contents

Introduction

storytelling is as old as the story of humanity itself. Every life is a story, and every story has a hidden message—a teaching. The saints, sadhus, and spiritual teachers of India have always used stories to explain concepts that words alone could not adequately convey. Stories captivate the listener emotionally as well as intellectually, providing a vivid environment in which teachings can come to life. Many of the stories in this collection were told to me by saints during the past half-century. Others are from the classic Hindu religious texts—the Puranas, Upanishads, and the famous scripture called the Mahabharata. These stories are ancient, but never become old. They reappear in different times and places—even different cultures—and in different forms, but their essence always remains the same. No one person can claim their authorship and so I do not say that these are my stories; they are eternal wisdom in story form, and I am their vessel.

To understand the wisdom within these stories it helps to understand the place of saints in Hindu life. The English word "saint" is derived from the Sanskrit word "sant," a combination of three sounds: sa, na, and ta. *Sa* stands for "santosh," which means contentment; *na* implies "namrita," meaning humility; and *ta* refers to "tyaga," renunciation. Thus, a saint is one who is content and humble and has renounced the world of physical pleasures. Renunciation occurs because the saint has learned that the purpose of life is to attain enlightenment, to have a face-to-face realization of Truth. He no longer has an interest in the illusory material world because total personal freedom can only be obtained by freeing oneself from the chains of earthly desires, thereby achieving unity of thought and action. Saints use many tools to help them achieve this freedom. Fasting, observing vows of silence or celibacy, sleeping less, chanting mantras, and performing breathing exercises all serve to disconnect the aspirant from the outer world, allowing more time to be devoted to the treasure inside. Saints who have renounced *all* material attachments, including that of a home, and wander the countryside, surviving on alms, are known as sadhus.

Detachment from the world of desires gives saints a unique role in Hindu culture. They exist outside the social hierarchy of the caste system. In fact, when an individual is initiated as a saint his family must perform funerary rites and rituals, as if he had died. A saint does not discriminate between high and low, rich and poor, pure and impure— everything is part of the same divine energy. This has allowed saints to exist as the traditional spiritual advisers of kings.

While saints take no interest in the world itself, they are quite interested in helping others to find the right path.

This, in fact, is their reason for being. Just as sympathetic vibration can carry over from one musical instrument to another, the inner peace and clarity of a saint can affect other beings, helping them to realize their own divine nature. Attachment to our senses keeps us from realizing this, and we become stuck in a cycle of reincarnation that continues life after life in a futile attempt to fulfill never-ending desires, until ego is finally destroyed. We are all moving toward enlightenment, and every lifetime holds the promise that some extraordinary event or effort will allow us to reach it. Saints, who have found the way and no longer labor on the path, help point the rest of us in the right direction.

Guiding others, however, is not always an easy task, as you will see in this collection. It is extremely difficult to destroy the ego and achieve inner stillness. I myself was an atheist and an empiricist, trusting only the truth that I could verify through my senses. The product of a well-reputed university, I was armed with many facts about the modern world. I had no respect for uneducated saints, who knew nothing of the modern world. I viewed them as parasites who did not contribute to society.

Bolstered by my master's degree in philosophy, I visited a saint to test my knowledge against his. In no time at all he made clear what I had not learned during my entire university experience—that everything I thought I knew and could explain with "real-world" examples I did not truly know. All I had done was memorize information and manipulate it in my head. Deep inside I had known I was a hypocrite all along.

This encounter changed my life, and I decided to devote myself to achieving true awareness. In the good company of saints I learned to be humble, patient, and true in word, deed, and thought. I came to understand that the best way to educate is to become an embodiment of the living teachings.

And the next best way is to embody the living teachings in stories.

As ship captains need lighthouses to find safe channels and harbors at night, so we need saints and their teaching stories to serve as beacons in the darkness, guiding us along paths that are far from clear. Humans are quite complex beings: born free, but everywhere in chains. We need models who have tamed the tiger of the mind and who, by living, teach. This is why India has always accepted the institution of saints. Living models of purity, service, devotion, harmony, and faith, they do not contribute to society in material ways but work on a higher level for humanity at large.

Every Indian knows that not everyone who dresses in saffron robes is a saint, not every person who embraces hardships is wise. Many criminals and beggars disguise themselves as saints to gain the goodwill of the populace, as do others who think they can survive on handouts by using such disguises. This has always been a drain on the social and economic health of India. But anyone whose eyes are truly open can easily distinguish a true saint from an impostor, for real saints have a calming effect on all beings, birds and beasts as well as humans. As it is said in a famous scripture, in the dwelling place of a saint the lions and goats drink water on the same beach.

A bird nesting in the banyan tree watched with great interest

The Bird of Prosperity

nce upon a time, in a remote village, lived a poor family. The man and his wife and their five children earned enough money to survive only by working hard for the other people of the village. One year the village was struck by a famine and everyone had to rely on whatever food they had put away. The poor man's family had lived hand to mouth for years and had no reserves, so he went to his neighbor, who owned a grove of fruit trees, and asked, "Friend, is there any work my family can do for you in exchange for some money or food?"

"Hah!" the neighbor laughed. "My trees are barren and I have no extra money. There is hardly enough for my own family. It's every man for himself this year."

It was the same story all over the village. The family had no choice but to move away and find jobs elsewhere. They left the village at dawn with some pots and straw mats, their only belongings. In the evening of the first day they stopped to camp in the jungle under a big banyan tree beside a river.

The younger children were exhausted by the day's walk and squatted on the jungle floor, holding their bellies with hunger. "We have to cook some food before it is dark," said the mother. She instructed her husband to build a fireplace and her two elder sons to gather wood and bring water from the river, while she worried about what to cook.

The family immediately went to work, each doing their assigned task, as they had learned from years of working together. In no time they had a pot of water boiling over a crackling fire. Unfortunately, the mother had not found anything she could cook for their supper.

A bird nesting in the banyan tree had watched all this with great interest. When he saw the family standing around the fire empty-handed he hopped onto a branch over their heads and chuckled. "You ignorant people! You have built a blazing fire and have nothing to put over it!"

Upon hearing the bird, the man and his eldest son's eyes met, and the son silently slipped around the other side of the banyan tree and began to climb it.

"You live in this jungle," the man said to the bird. "Don't you know something we can eat?"

"Just bugs and worms," said the bird. "Bugs and worms. That's what I eat. I don't know about people food. Guess you'll starve."

"Then perhaps you know of a nearby village where we might find help."

"No villages for days on your slow feet," said the bird. "Guess you'll—" and this was all the bird said, for the eldest son had crept up from behind and wrapped a straw mat around him.

"We will cook you!" said the son. "Foolish bird, you think you can mock my family?" He climbed down and prepared to throw the bird into the cooking pot.

"Please don't eat me!" begged the bird. "Spare me, and I will bring you to a place where you will find much tastier fare than me."

"If you swear it," said the father, "then we will trust your honor."

"I swear it," said the bird. They let him go. "Follow me," he said.

The elder sons followed the bird through the jungle while the others stayed back to watch the fire. Soon he led them to a clearing where a mango tree rose fifty feet into the air and dropped its heavy fruit to the ground by the hundreds.

"O wonderful bird," cried the sons, "we are saved!" They held the fruit to their noses, inhaling the spicy perfume, and began filling their mats with mangos.

"But why don't you eat any?" asked the bird. "I know you are starving."

"That wouldn't be fair to the others," said the eldest son. "We must get this food back as quickly as possible. Then we all can eat."

"You are truly a good family," said the bird. "Because of your love for each other and your cooperation, I will show you an old treasure." With his wing he pointed to the root of the mango tree. "Dig in that spot and you will find prosperity to match your industriousness."

The sons had nothing with which to dig, but one found the shell of a river turtle and the other found a long, straight piece of wood and a vine, and they soon created a shovel. After a few minutes of digging they uncovered a pot filled with rubies. They looked at each other in astonishment, filled their pockets with the gems, and rushed back to their family with all that they had found.

Overjoyed by their good fortune, the family ate mangos until they were stuffed and their faces and hands were sticky.

They uncovered a pot filled with rubies

In the morning they walked back to the village with their rubies. They sold one ruby and used the money to fix the roof of their house. They sold another and bought a dozen small fruit trees and a cow. They sold a third and bought sacks of grain and fruit and spices and bottles of coconut oil.

Their neighbor saw the changes in the poor man's household and asked the man what had happened. The man told him of the bird in the banyan tree and how it had led them to the rubies.

This is fantastic, thought the neighbor. If he can do it, so can I.

The next day, before dawn, the neighbor told his wife and children that they all had to leave town immediately and walk all day into the jungle. "Why should we?" said his children. "We have other things we'd rather do."

"Because I said so," said the neighbor. He forced them out of the house and they marched grumbling all day until they reached the banyan tree by the riverbank. Exhausted, the three sons fell to the ground.

"Quickly," said the wife, "one of you boys must gather

firewood and another must get water from the river."

"Not me," said the eldest son, "I didn't want to come in the first place. Let my brothers do it."

"I couldn't get up if the jungle itself was on fire," said the middle son. "Leave me here to rest."

"I'm the smallest and weakest," said the youngest son. "I shouldn't be the one to do the chores."

The argument continued, with none of the sons moving from their spot, and the sun began to set. The neighbor tried to settle the dispute. "You will all go and do the chores," he said. "I am your father, and you will obey my orders."

"Hah!" they laughed at him. "Why should we? It was your stupid idea to come out here, so why don't you get the wood and the water."

The wife grew angry at her entire family. "I can't believe this. It is getting dark and we haven't made any progress. We won't have anything to eat until we get a fire going and water boiling, so who is going to take the lead? It certainly won't be me, because I'll be doing the cooking."

They all looked at each other and waited. No one was about to let the others take advantage of their generosity.

The bird in the banyan tree had watched all this with great interest. He said, "Foolish people! You have no water and no fire. The sun is setting. What will you eat?"

"We will eat you!" said the eldest son, glaring at the bird.

"And how will you do that?" asked the bird. "Who will take the lead?"

The family looked at each other uncertainly.

"Those who can catch me are of one mind, and do not think of themselves. They cooperate, respect their parents, and care for their children." Saying this, the bird of prosperity flew away with the last ray of the setting sun, and the hungry family was swallowed by darkness.

People piled all their iron into carts

The Secret Formula

nce upon a time a prized statue was stolen from the palace of a king. The three thieves were apprehended, convicted, and the king sentenced them to be hanged. The first two thieves marched to the gallows without a word, weeping softly, and were hanged, but as the hangman took the third thief to the scaffold and slipped the noose around his neck, the thief begged for an extension of his life.

"On what grounds?" asked the hangman.

"I know a secret formula," said the thief, "that can make the world prosperous and happy. I need to share this alchemy with someone, so that the secret science does not die with me."

"Very well," said the hangman. "Tell me the formula."

"Oh, no. This secret is too important for any but the

king's ears. Please bring him to me."

"Nonsense. The king does not come to see thieves. I will kill you now."

"Do you really want to live the rest of your life knowing that you allowed a secret that could benefit all humanity to die? And what if the king discovered this?"

The hangman thought about the thief's words. To be safe, he informed the king of the thief's claim. As the king was a man who was interested in both wealth and the good of his kingdom, he agreed to talk with the thief. He went to the scaffold, where the thief still stood with the noose around his neck.

"All right, thief," the king said. "I am here. What is your secret formula?"

"It changes iron into gold, my lord," said the thief.

"Excellent!" said the king. "Tell me how."

"It is as easy as chanting a sacred mantra," said the thief. "But you must also sprinkle the juice of a rare herb over the iron. The herb is only found in high valleys in the Himalayas."

"Tell me the name of the herb and I will send my couriers at once to gather it."

"It is so rare that it has no name. I only know it by sight. It would be best for me to gather it and bring it back to you."

The king laughed. "Do you think I'm a fool? As soon as you were outside the kingdom we would never see you again. I will send a garrison of soldiers to accompany you. If you make any effort to escape, they will kill you instantly. If you can't find this herb, they will also kill you."

"Very well," said the thief. "But while I am gone, please announce the secret to the kingdom, and tell everyone to come to the palace with all the iron they own. The miracle becomes more powerful with every extra soul that chants the mantra."

The thief was sent to the Himalayas with a garrison of soldiers and a number of carts to collect as much of the herb as possible. Meanwhile, the announcement caused a surge of excitement in the kingdom. People dropped their chores and piled all their iron tools into carts, even pulled nails out of their houses. Soon the palace courtyard was packed with the king's subjects and piles of horseshoes, cooking pots, swords, and other iron items. All eagerly awaited the return of the thief.

Just as the people were beginning to grow restless, the doors to the courtyard opened and in rode the thief and the soldiers, pulling carts filled with strange silvery-green leaves. A ripple of excitement went through the crowd as the thief, carrying a sprig of the herb, climbed onto the stage where the king waited with an iron pot.

The thief began chanting the mantra. They all recognized it instantly and joined in. When it was complete, the thief held up the herb. "My lord, the juice of this herb can now be sprinkled over the iron to convert it to gold. But

The thief began chanting the mantra

there is one condition: only one who is so pure as to never have stolen from the day of his birth can sprinkle the juice. Obviously, I cannot do it. But I'm sure that you, as a king, are pure enough."

"Of course," said the king. He took the herb from the thief, crushed it, and let the juice fall on the pot. Everyone waited. Nothing happened. "What is wrong?" asked the king.

"I don't know," said the thief. "Everything is in place. Are you certain you have never stolen?"

The king thought for a moment. His face flushed with embarassment. "I have stolen," he said. A gasp of shock went through the crowd. "I once stole sweets from my mother's cupboard. I was ill and was forbidden to eat any-thing. But one night I was so hungry that I stole the sweets. I had never told anyone until this day."

"There is the problem," said the thief. "But surely there is one among your subjects who has never stolen."

"Yes," said the king, turning to the crowd. "Let one who has never stolen come forward."

At first no one came forward. Finally, an old woman wearing only rags slowly made her way to the stage. She was known throughout the kingdom for a life devoted entirely to austerity and good deeds. The thief handed her another sprig and she crushed the juice over the pot. Again nothing happened.

"Think hard," said the thief. "Are you certain you have never stolen?"

The woman closed her eyes for a very long time. At last she opened them and said, "Once, while I was walking in the woods, I saw a sparrow that had found a lovely piece of golden lace and woven it into its nest. I scared the sparrow off and took the lace."

The thief shook his head. "Then you have stolen, too."

"But a sparrow—" said the woman.

"It does not matter," said the thief.

"Somebody else," said the king. "Somebody who has never stolen come forward."

No one came forward.

The thief folded his hands and looked at the king. "Then my lord," he said, "why would you hang me, when everyone in your kingdom is a thief?"

The sweeper was completely unaware of the princess

The Sweeper Who Became a Saint

nce upon a time in Central India there was a sweeper who cleaned the outside toilet used by male members of the royal family. His wife cleaned the inside toilet used by the ladies. One day the sweeper's wife was ill and he had to clean the inside toilet as well. In so doing he happened to catch a glimpse of the princess. He was stunned by her beauty and instantly fell in love.

All that day the sweeper could not get the thought of the princess out of his mind. He went home but did not say anything to his wife. That night he could not sleep. He lay staring at the ceiling. The thought that he would probably never see her again made him sick. As time went by his pain grew and he lost his appetite.

The sweeper's wife noticed the changes in her husband and asked what was wrong. The sweeper did not wish to upset his wife, but he could contain himself no longer. "I am afraid I am in love with the princess," he said. "I think I will die if I do not see her again."

At this his wife burst into tears and became very angry. But she could see how miserable her husband was and after a while she asked, "Do you really think you will die if you do not see her?"

"Yes," moaned the sweeper.

"Then I will help you. I will pretend to be sick, and you can go to the inner palace and clean."

They did this for several days. At first the sweeper was ecstatic to glimpse the princess again, and for a few moments his pain faded. But soon just stealing glances at her was not enough. His desire to speak with her and have her know him became more and more intense.

Eventually the sweeper said to his wife, "Somehow you must arrange for me to meet with the princess. Just one meeting, and then I think we can live in peace."

His wife sighed. "I will try."

She returned to her job, and one day when the princess was alone in the courtyard she summoned up her courage and approached. "My Lady," she said, "what I am about to tell you embarasses me greatly, but I must speak. My husband, who also works at the palace, has fallen in love with you and says that he will die unless you meet with him."

The princess was stunned by the woman's words and could not speak.

"If you will only meet with him once, and say a few kind words, I think he will be all right."

At last the princess said, "What you ask is impossible. It would not be allowed for me to meet alone with a commoner. But here is what I can do. Tell your husband to go to the temple of Maheshwari Devi on Thursday, the day my family and I bring the saints food and gifts. Tell him to dress like a saint and sit with the other saints. I have noticed your

Soon just stealing glances at her was not enough

husband watching me and will look for him. Then he can eat food from my hand and speak a few words with me."

The sweeper's wife thanked the princess for her generosity and went home to deliver the news to her beloved husband. The sweeper was overjoyed and could hardly wait for Thursday, when he would at last meet his beloved princess.

On Thursday morning he awoke very early, dressed himself in the saffron robes of a saint, and went to the temple of Maheshwari Devi. He was the first to arrive. Slowly saints from the surrounding area gathered in the temple courtyard. The sweeper feared that they would instantly recognize him as an impostor and throw him out, but they paid him no mind at all. Each sat in a lotus posture and began chanting a mantra.

The sweeper copied the posture of a saint sitting nearby. He knew nothing of mantras, but he knew he needed to chant something to fit in. All he could think of was the name of Lord Ram, so he began chanting "Shri Ram Jai

Ram Jai Jai Ram" over and over again.

In his mind the sweeper played out scenarios of his meeting with the princess—what she would say, what he would say back. He could hardly stand to wait. After about an hour he exhausted his fantasies and instead began to notice how uncomfortable it was to stay in the same position so long. He knew there were still hours before the princess and her family arrived.

The drone of the saints' mantras became a rhythmic pulsing inside him, and he stopped being able to differentiate the words. His own chant had become automatic, something he could only have stopped with great effort. "Shri Ram Jai Ram Jai Jai Ram" went his head.

After a while the sweeper lost all feeling in his body, and he no longer felt so uncomfortable. For hours the vibrating mantras went on. Time passed so slowly that he forgot where he was or why he had come. He only knew the vibrations that were outside and within him at the same time. Quite without knowing it he entered into a state of samadhi.

It was then that the royal coach arrived. The princess stepped from the carriage and moved among the saints, handing out food and clothes. She saw the sweeper and when the other members of her family were not looking she came up next to him. "I have come to you," she whispered. "Now open your eyes and take this food from me."

The sweeper was completely unaware of the princess. She repeated her words, but he remained frozen. "Please," she said, nudging his shoulder, "I am risking a lot. Open your eyes and speak to me." Still he took no notice. At last she gave up and went inside the temple to worship with the rest of her family. When she came out all the saints were gone. Only the sweeper remained in his saffron robe, unchanged from when she had left him. "Everybody is gone," she said to him. "You must go home now." She might as well have spoken to a post. Eventually she also went away.

At sunset the sweeper's wife came to find him. She saw him sitting silently and said, "It is almost dark. What are you doing? Get up and come home." Getting no reaction, she leaned down and shook him by the shoulders.

At this he opened his eyes and stared blankly at her. He opened his mouth and said, "Shri Ram Jai Ram Jai Jai Ram."

"What is wrong with you?" she shouted. "What happened with the princess? Why won't you get up and come home?"

In a faraway voice he said, "Shri Ram Jai Ram Jai Jai Ram."

Finally his wife burst into tears. "I have done so much for you," she said, "and this is the thanks I get? Our children are all alone and will get frightened if we don't get home by nightfall."

All her efforts were in vain, however. As she could not carry him, she returned to her children alone. The sweeper remained in samadhi all through the night, and early the next morning he left his mortal body.

As was customary, the boy came to visit the saint

Transformation

Once there was a boy named Bachchu who lived in a village in northern India. He was a great devotee of Baba Santosh Dass, who lived a very simple life in a hut outside of town. One day Bachchu went to Baba and told him that the village chief had found a job for him in a nearby village, and he would soon be leaving. The saint blessed the boy and wished him luck.

One year later some friends of Bachchu's came to Baba and said that Bachchu had fallen in with a bad group of boys in the nearby village and was now stealing for a living. The saint heard this with great surprise, for he knew Bachchu to be a good person at heart. He thanked the friends for this information, but said nothing else.

Shortly after that Bachchu returned home to visit his family. As was customary, he came to visit the saint.

"And how is your life in your new town, Bachchu?" the saint asked.

"Very good, Baba," the boy replied.

"Are you enjoying your job?"

"I no longer have that job, Baba. I met a group of people who gave me a much better job that is not so boring."

"I am pleased to hear it. Since you are doing so well, I would like to visit you in your new home."

The boy looked startled, but he said, "I am honored, Baba."

"As you know, I can assume any form I choose. Since you have known me all your life, I still expect you to recognize me. Will you know me when I come?"

"I will know you, Baba, in whatever form you come."

Bachchu returned to his new town. His friends greeted him and said, "Hey Bachchu, come with us. We're going to lift some money from people at the village market."

"Sure," said Bachchu. When he got to the village market he saw a well-dressed stranger paying for some loaves of bread with a large pouch of money. Bachchu followed the stranger to several other stalls and saw where the stranger carried his pouch. He walked up, timing it so that he could grab the pouch and run as soon as the stranger took it out, but suddenly he thought, "What if this is Baba? He would never forgive me for stealing," and he stayed back.

On their way back to their home Bachchu's friends asked him why he had not gotten any money and Bachchu replied that he had been about to make his move when a policeman had come by. When they turned the corner onto their street the gang saw an old man who had just fallen under the weight of the apples he was carrying back from market. Apples had spilled all over the street. Bachchu knew the gang was about to run and grab the apples, and he thought, "This, too, could be Baba. From the time I was a small boy he has taught me to help those in need," and before the rest of the gang knew what he was doing Bachchu came forward and helped the old man up, then collected all his apples and put them back in his sack.

The old man touched him warmly on the shoulder and said, "Thank you for such kindness, young man," and went on his way. Bachchu felt a change inside himself. The old man was not Baba, but he was still someone in need, and Bachchu remembered how good it felt to help others. From then on every face he saw, every bird and every tree, he knew might be Baba. He began to see the world in a very different way and treat it all with the reverence he had formerly reserved for his old teacher. His friends became suspicious of his actions, and gradually he stopped associating with them. He found a new job and became a valued member of the village.

A year later Bachchu's old friends again visited Baba. They thanked him and asked him what he had done to turn the boy around so quickly.

Baba said, "It was not me. He changed himself. I simply gave him a new perspective, and I am sure that if anyone sees God in every creature, their whole world will change. And if everyone practices this, the whole world *will* change."

The saint began feeling through the milk with his hand

The Butter in the Milk

ne day a young aspirant went to see an old saint who lived beside a river in a small hut made of hemp sacks and bamboo poles. The simple atmosphere of the hut calmed the aspirant's mind and he enjoyed the company of the saint very much. When the time came to leave, the young man asked the saint if he could ask him an important question.

"Of course, my son," said the saint.

"Where can I find God?"

The saint smiled. "That is not an easy question. Allow me to dwell on it. Come again tomorrow and I will answer it. Also, please bring a glass of milk."

The young man agreed and went home, excited that the next day his question would be answered. He thought it odd that the saint requested a glass of milk, but it was a simple request to fulfill, so the next day he returned with the glass of milk.

The saint thanked him for the milk and poured it into his begging bowl. Then he put his fingers in the milk and lifted them up, but when the milk ran through them he frowned and repeated the gesture, with the same result.

The young man watched, perplexed, but remained silent. He wished the saint would finish with this foolishness and get on to his question.

The saint began feeling through the milk with his hand, occasionally lifting his hand out and staring in his palm, but when he saw his palm was empty he would return to fishing through the milk.

At last the young man's patience was gone and he said, "Guruji, what are you looking for?"

"I have heard that there is butter in milk," said the saint. "I am searching for the butter."

Before he could stop himself the young man laughed and said, "It is not like that. The butter is not separate from the milk, it is a part of it. You have to convert the milk to yogurt and then churn it to make the butter come out."

"Very good!" said the saint. "I believe you have the answer to your question." And he quaffed the bowl of milk in one long drink. "Now go and churn the milk of your soul until you have found God."

He pulled his soaking body up the rope

The Merchant and
the Courtesan

nce upon a time there was a young and
prosperous merchant named
Bilvamangal. He was madly in love with
a courtesan named Chintamani, with
whom he spent many nights in her
home across the river. One evening
during the rainy season Bilvamangal closed his shop and
went down to the river to find a boatman to take him
across. All day he had dreamed of Chintamani and he could
hardly wait to be with her. The rainy season in India is
famous for making people romantic.

When Bilvamangal reached the docks he found that the
rains had swelled the river, which surged over its banks and
covered half the docks. He went up to the first boatman he
saw and asked to be ferried across, but the boatman said,
"Are you kidding? We would be swept to our deaths for
sure. Nothing can cross the river."

"But I must see my beloved," said Bilvamangal.

"It is too dark and too rough. You will have to wait."

Bilvamangal searched for another boatman to carry him across the river, but they had all gone home to wait out the storm. He paced up and down the docks, rain pounding in his eyes. All he could think of was Chintamani, Chintamani, Chintamani. He pictured her in her bed, waiting for him. In his head he could envision her beautiful body and her gorgeous dancing. He peered into the inky blackness. Though he could see nothing he could hear the thundering river.

At midnight he could stand it no longer. "I must see my beloved!" he said to himself, "whatever the risks." He leaped into the river and began swimming across.

Instantly the current swept Bilvamangal downstream, and though he pulled with a superhuman strength he was no match for it. The churning waters pulled him under again and again, and each time he could barely claw his way to the surface for another breath.

Just when he was about to give up and be pulled underwater forever he was swept into something floating in the river. "A log," he thought, "I am saved! I will reach my beloved after all." He pulled himself up on the spongy surface and caught his breath. In his mind he could hear Chintamani's lovely voice, singing. Desire welled up in him and he paddled across the river with a strength he did not know he possessed.

When he reached the other side he pulled the log up on the shore so that he could use it to return the next day. Rain still pounding on his exhausted body, he dragged himself to Chintamani's house. All was dark inside. When he tried the door, it was locked. He knocked, but there was no answer. Thinking that she must be asleep, he went around to the other side of the house, but the back door was locked as well.

"How terrible!" he said to himself. "I have come all this

He paddled across the river

way and now I cannot get inside." He walked all around the house, searching for a way in. In the darkness he saw a long, thin shape hanging down from the balcony of Chintamani's bedroom. "How nice," he thought. "She has left a rope so that I may climb into her room." The romantic gesture made his heart swell with love. He pulled his soaking body up the rope with the last of his strength.

When he entered her bedroom Chintamani was sleeping. In the dark he could just make out her beautiful face, and he felt the heat of love fill his body. He walked over to her bed and leaned over her face. Drops of water fell from his hair onto her cheek. She opened her eyes and stared into his face. She sat up, astonished, and said, "Bilvamangal! I never thought you would come. How could you make it here through the storm?"

"Nothing can keep me from you," said Bilvamangal. "My love conquers all obstacles. I jumped into the river to swim across to you and was helped by a log that came floating by. Then I climbed up the rope you left for me and came to your side."

"Rope?" said Chintamani. "I did not leave any rope."

"You must have. It is hanging from your balcony right now."

"I would like to see it." Chintamani lit her oil lamp and followed Bilvamangal to the balcony. She held the lamp out and there, its tail twisted around the balcony rail, was a huge cobra hanging down, stiff from the cold storm.

"Oh my god!" said Chintamani. She stared at Bilvamangal. "You could have been killed! Could you not tell a clammy snake from a soft rope?"

"I wasn't thinking about it," said an equally shocked Bilvamangal. "It was so dark, and I was only thinking of you."

"You had better show me the log," said Chintamani.

Together they walked through the rain to the riverbank. Chintamani held her lamp over the dark shape Bilvamangal pointed to and screamed. There was the body of a peasant who had drowned in the river. "You couldn't tell a dead body from a log?" she said, shaking. "Are you completely blinded by love?"

"I just wanted to reach you," said Bilvamangal meekly. "I love you so."

Chintamani embraced Bilvamangal and said, "I am not worthy of such love. I am a courtesan. You love me for my beauty alone. My body is impure, but your love is pure. Only God is worthy of a love as intense as yours. If you loved Him as you do me, Bilvamangal, I believe you would find him."

Bilvamangal listened to her words, and stared at the dead body and the raging river he had crossed. He watched the surging black waves, and saw the ghost of a hand in every one. "Say it again, my love," he said.

Chintamani repeated her words. "It is God who got you through," she said. "Not me."

Bilvamangal watched the frothing waves and saw the ghost of a face in every one. He understood that he had not

"I am not worthy of such love"

found the body by accident, and the snake had not come to
that balcony by chance. "Say it again, my love," he said.

Chintamani repeated her words a third time. Bilvamangal
heard the words, but it was not her he heard speak, and his
whole being underwent a transformation. He folded his
hands in reverence and said, "You have awakened me at last,
dear woman. You have kindled the flame of divine love in
my heart. I will love God as madly as I ever loved you.
Thank you so much." And with that he bowed to touch her
feet and left.

Bilvamangal became a follower of Krishna, the lord of
love, and joined a monastery. He spent each day praying
and fervently reciting the name of Krishna.

One day, as he was cleaning the temple courtyard while
repeating a mantra, he caught a glimpse of a lady leaving
the temple. By her long, dark hair and her dress he was certain it was Chintamani. Memories flooded him and he forgot his mantra entirely. He rushed out of the temple and
followed her through the streets. When she reached her
house the woman turned around and said, "May I help you,
Sir?" It was not Chintamani at all.

The old feelings that had welled up in Bilvamangal sub-sided. "Would you be so kind as to bring me two needles, dear lady," he asked.

The woman went into her house and came back with two needles. Bilvamangal took the needles and thanked her. "Eyes are a great hindrance in my path," he said. "Only blind madness will allow me to reach God." And with that he pricked out both his eyes.

Bilvamangal became a blind poet, and never forgot a mantra again.

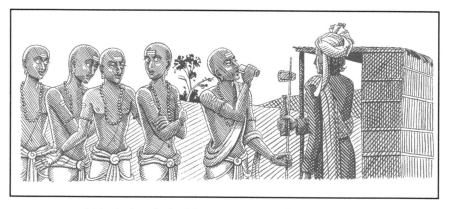

"Alcohol is forbidden, yet our teacher drinks it"

Shankara and His Disciples

he saint Shankara was once traveling with his disciples in the forest in north-western India. It was one of the hottest days of an extremely hot summer, and Shankara had allowed his disciples to drink their entire supply of water with-out using any himself. Eventually he grew thirsty and asked his disciples to find some water for him to drink, but they searched for miles in all directions and could not find a sin-gle spring or brook. Just when Shankara thought he would collapse of thirst he saw a hut in a clearing with people sit-ting around it, drinking from bottles.

Shankara and his disciples approached the hut and Shankara said, "Brothers, I am very thirsty. Could you please spare a little water to drink?"

The people laughed drunkenly and one of them said, "Sorry, no water here. This is wine, but you're welcome to it."

Shankara thought for a moment and said, "All right, then, I would graciously accept a glass of wine, as my throat is cracking with dryness."

One of the people filled a glass with wine and handed it to Shankara. He drained it in one motion, thanked the people for their kindness, and left.

His disciples stared in astonishment. They looked at each other and said, "Alcohol is forbidden, yet our teacher drinks it!"

In the evening they reached a village and stopped at a shelter that was used by pilgrims. Leaving Shankara resting under a banyan tree, the disciples went into the town to get food. They stepped into a tavern and saw people at the bar drinking wine. "Why not?" they said to themselves. "If it is all right for our teacher, it must be all right for us, too." They proceeded to order glass after glass.

Shankara noticed his disciples stumbling drunkenly into the shelter that night, but he pretended to be asleep. Many of them were sick all night.

The next morning Shankara rose very early and expressed his desire to visit the shrine of the goddess Durga, which was in a desert near the village. His disciples all had headaches and did not rouse easily. When he had them all on their feet they started into the desert together. The day grew fiery and the sand burned under their feet. Soon they finished all the water they were carrying. The disciples felt ill and dehydrated and thought they would soon collapse in the desert.

Just then they saw a group of people boiling something in a pot over a fire. They approached the group and Shankara said, "Brothers, my disciples and I are parched to the bone. Do you have any water to spare?"

"Sorry," said one of the group, "we have no water. We are boiling lead in this pot to make weapons."

Shankara thought for a minute and then said, "All right, then. May I have some boiling lead?"

The man stared at him and said, "If you like."

Shankara cupped his palms together and dipped them into the boiling lead. He brought his palms to his lips and drank the molten lead down in one gulp. Smacking his lips in satisfaction, Shankara turned to his disciples and said, "Come, who is next?"

The disciples shrank back, staring at their teacher in horror.

"Are you not dying of thirst?" said Shankara. "Come forward and do as I did."

"But Master, it is boiling lead!" said a disciple. "How can we drink it?"

"But you drank alcohol last night. What is the difference?"

"Alcohol is one thing, but boiling lead? We would surely die!"

"Why do you discriminate?" said Shankara. "It is all the same, all divine energy. Have you forgotten your lessons? This discrimination into different things is an illusory act of the mind. There is but one essence, Brahman, who is water and wine and lead and all else. Did I not teach you this?"

"You did, Master, but our senses tell us otherwise."

"Then why did you think it would be acceptable to drink alcohol last night? If lead is lead and water is water, then liquor is liquor. When you can comfortably drink lead then you can also drink liquor for water. Until then, that which is forbidden must remain forbidden, no matter how harmless it seems. The liquor you drank has hurt your souls as much as boiling lead would hurt your bellies."

The disciples saw their error and were ashamed. "We are sorry, Master," they cried. "Please tell us what penance we can do to make up for our mistake."

"You are doing it right now," said Shankara, as the disciples' bodies burned in the desert air and their heads throbbed with their night's transgression.

"I will leave you two wise men alone"

What to Do When You Meet a Fool

nce upon a time a clever son was born to a slow-witted father. With time the son grew up, educated himself, and became well-known for his wit and presence of mind. Stories of his wisdom reached the king, who appointed him to be a minister in the palace. The new minister was very successful and quickly solved problems that had perplexed the king for years. He learned that the king fancied himself the wisest man in all the kingdom, and he became quite adept at making the king think he had come up with these clever ideas himself.

One day the king said to the minister, "You are very wise, almost as wise as me. Your father must have been an incredibly wise man to have raised such a son as you."

"Indeed, your Highness, he is practically a sage," said the minister, knowing that if the king knew his father to be slow, he would think less of the minister.

"I should like to meet him," said the king. "We would have many interesting things to discuss."

Knowing that the king's mind was not easily changed, the minister said, "I shall arrange a time for the two of you to meet."

The minister went to his elderly father, who now lived with him, and said, "Father, the king would like to meet with you. When you meet, please greet him with respect but after that do not respond to any of his questions unless you are completely sure of your answer." His father agreed and the minister returned to the king and said, "My father would be honored to meet with you tomorrow."

The next day, after finishing his morning prayers, the king proceeded to the house of the minister without bodyguards or servants, accompanied only by the minister himself. When they arrived the minister's youngest son presented the king with a garland of flowers. Then the minister led the king into the room where his father was sitting, bowed to them both, said, "I will leave you two wise men alone to get to know each other," and departed.

The two men were pleased by the respect shown by the minister, and they greeted each other with smiles. Immediately, the king said, "I would like to hear your words of wisdom on any advice you think I should have."

The minister's father was quite overwhelmed by the question and decided this was one he should not answer.

After waiting for several minutes, the king said, "What do you think is the greatest problem facing the kingdom?"

The father knew there were many problems but he had no idea which was the greatest, so again he remained silent.

After waiting again, the king said, "Would you like to hear the wisest things I have learned from my years of rulership?"

The father was certain he would not be able to understand such things, but did not want to insult the king by saying no. Uncertain which was the correct answer, he said nothing.

The king waited and grew uncomfortable. "How did you teach your son to be so wise?" he asked.

The old man remained silent.

"What does it feel like to be old?"

Still the old man was silent.

The king thought, Either this man is very wise or very foolish, but I have no idea which. Frustrated, he said his goodbye and left the room. The minister, waiting outside, accompanied the king back to the royal palace. As they were walking the king asked, "What should you do when you meet a fool?"

"You should remain silent, your Highness," said the minister, who then became silent himself.

A falcon landed on his shoulder

The King
of a Year

nce upon a time, on the bank of a wide river, there was a city that chose its king with the help of a falcon. On the summer solstice the people would march through the streets, beating drums and singing songs. A falcon would be released over the crowd and whomever it touched was declared king. On the last day of the year the leading citizens of the city would take the king, row him across the river, and abandon him on the far bank. Then a new king would be chosen.

It so happened that on the solstice a stranger had just arrived in the city. He walked the streets, hearing the sounds of drums and shouts and thinking that he must have arrived just in time for some festival. He turned the corner and saw the crowd heading straight for him. Before he knew what was happening, a falcon landed on his shoulder.

"The king is found! The king is found!" the crowd shouted with joy. The high priest and the prime minister of the city came forward and saluted him.

"What is going on?" asked the stranger.

"You are now our king," said the prime minister, "because the holy bird touched you."

"Me? King? But I am a newcomer. How can I rule people whom I know nothing about?"

"The government and the church are already taken care of," said the high priest. "All you need to do is preside over ceremonies and give the people someone to look up to. You will enjoy it."

"But I don't want to," said the stranger.

"You have no choice. You have been chosen by the holy bird. It is the law of the gods. Thus it has been for hundreds of years."

Before the stranger could say anything more, the crowd began chanting, "Long live the king! Long live the king!" The next thing he knew they had swept him into a golden palanquin and carried him to the royal palace.

At the palace the stranger was received by a group of beautiful maid servants who led him inside, bathed him, anointed him with oil and sweet herbs, and dressed him in the royal robes. The stranger began thinking that it might not be such a bad thing to be the king. Afterward he was led to the royal court, where the crowd had gathered. He was crowned and seated on his throne, and a grand feast began that lasted through the night. He was introduced to his five queens, and everyone presented him with beautiful gifts.

The next morning the prime minister said to the new king, "So, your majesty, what do you think of being king?"

"It is wonderful," said the king. "I can't believe my good fortune."

"Indeed, it will be the best year of your life."

"What do you mean year?"

"We choose our king for one year. On the last day of the year we will take you across the river and choose a new king."

The king grew alarmed. "What is on the other side of the river?"

"No one knows, your majesty. It is forbidden to go there, and none of the old kings have ever returned."

"And the kings always go willingly?"

"It is the law of the gods. Why would we question it? If we broke the law, misfortune might befall the city. But we give the king no choice."

The king was very disturbed, and the first chance he got he went to the riverbank and peered toward the other side. The river was so wide that he could only make out a thin line on the other side, and even this was obscured by mist. Over the days he looked again and again, but the far bank seemed to be forever lost in mist.

The king worried greatly what would happen to him after his year, but he was entertained by a constant stream of magicians, singers, and actors who wished to perform for the king, and he found it difficult to keep his mind on something so far in the future. When he wasn't watching entertainers he was hosting lavish banquets, speaking with the people, being massaged by servants, or enjoying the company of his five queens. The royal gardeners left flowers on his bed each night, and the palace always smelled sweetly. Each day was an unending parade of delights, and he yielded to them easily.

His new life was so vivid that after forty days of being king it eclipsed his old, uneventful life entirely, and he quite forgot about his family and homeland. But as fall passed he began to notice that the people of the city were so caught up in their official festivals, rules, and physical delights that, other than his palace, the city was quite run down, and little was ever accomplished.

One day while sitting in the royal garden with one of his

queens, the king asked, "Do you think I could improve the way the city is run?"

"What an odd question," said the queen. "The city is as it will always be."

"Do you think it is fair that I will be taken to the far side of the river at the end of this year?"

"Fair? What do you mean? That is what happens to the king."

"Have you ever wondered what is on the other side?"

"Of course not. It is forbidden."

Frustrated, the king left his queen sitting there and walked through the garden. Fruit trees of all kinds surrounded him, heavy with fat fruit. The entire garden was perfectly weeded and bursting with good health, such a contrast to the rest of the city. The king turned a corner and found the chief gardener on his hands and knees, planting bulbs.

"Why bother with that now?" said the king. "They won't come up before the frost."

"Preparing for winter is perhaps the most important part of gardening. If I put the bulbs in now, your majesty, they will do wonderfully come the spring."

"Your gardens are so beautiful," said the king. "You and your assistants obviously care for them."

"We do, your majesty. Every year they give me new joy."

The king found the gardener very refreshing, and through the fall he spent more and more time with him. He watched as the gardener spent many hours cutting the dead growth, planting bulbs, and adding fertilizer for the following year.

"Don't you mind spending so much time in the cold, when nothing is growing anymore?" the king asked the gardener one day.

"In some ways it is my favorite time to be here," his friend answered. "It is peaceful and allows me to think, and

I love anticipating the new growth."

"You are very wise," said the king. "Do you think it is fair that I will be taken to the far side of the river at the end of this year?"

"It is the law," said the gardener uncomfortably.

"Do you think it is fair?"

"I think it is good to know what the new year brings," said the gardener, and he would say no more.

One cold fall morning the king slipped out of the palace and took a small rowboat across the river. An icy wind blew down the huge river and the king rowed in and out of waves. At last he reached the far shore, glided through the mist, and pulled his boat up on the bank.

A dripping, black forest awaited him, so dense he could hardly find his way through it. Branches clutched at him and his path closed up behind him as quickly as he made it. Tangled in the trees were the skeletons of previous kings. There were no people living on the far side of the river, and there was no shelter.

The king returned to the city before anyone knew he was gone, but as the days lengthened the gardener noticed how depressed he had become, and asked him what was wrong.

"I have seen the other side," said the king, "and I do not wish to go there."

"But you have no choice. All kings must go there. If you did not, it might bring ruin on the city."

The king did not wish to bring misfortune to the city. He took the gardener into his confidence, and asked him to help with a secret plan.

No one but the king noticed that spring that the chief gardener was missing from the royal gardens. On the morning of the summer solstice, the leading citizens of the city burst into the royal palace, held the king by the neck, and brought him down to a boat. The king did not struggle. They rowed across the river and left him on the far bank.

The king did not struggle

The king watched the boat depart, then turned to the
dark forest. A new trail was cut through it. He followed the
trail to a clearing, and there stood a small, well-made house.
Beside it his faithful servant and true friend, the gardener,
welcomed him. Radiant poppies were already blooming near
the door.

He lifted the bedraggled scorpion in his palm

The Saint and
the Scorpion

ne day a saint was taking a bath in a river. His disciple sat on the bank with the saint's clothes, asana, and rosary. The saint noticed a scorpion struggling in the current. Taking pity, he lifted the bedraggled scorpion in his palm and started wading toward the bank.

No sooner had the scorpion recovered than it promptly stung the saint on the palm. The saint felt an unbearable, burning pain shoot up his arm, but he did not drop the scorpion. Instead, he gently shook his hand to encourage the scorpion to move away from the wound.

The saint's disciple, watching from the bank, became alarmed, but did not say anything.

The saint had only taken a few more steps when the scorpion stung him again. A searing pain more intense than the first one went all the way up his arm and throbbed in his head. The saint staggered and nearly collapsed in the river.

This time the disciple did call out. "Put him down, Guruji! He will only sting you again. Leave him to his fate. Your kindness is of no value to such a creature. He will learn nothing from it!"

The saint ignored him and continued walking. He had nearly reached the bank when the scorpion stung him for a third time. The pain exploded into his head, lungs, and heart. The disciple saw a blissful smile appear on the saint's face before he collapsed into the river. The disciple dragged the saint to the shore, still smiling and still cradling the scorpion in his palm. As soon as they had reached shore, the scorpion crawled away as quickly as it could.

"Guruji!" said the disciple after the saint had regained consciousness. "How can you smile? That wretched creature nearly killed you."

"You are right, my son," said the saint. "But he was only following his dharma, his nature. It is the dharma of a scorpion to sting, and it is the dharma of a saint to save its life. He is following his dharma and I am following mine. Everything is in its proper place. That is why I am so happy."

Everyone waited to see what Dhapli Baba would do

Dhapli Baba

n a small town there lived a saint by the name of Dhapli Baba. He was called this because he was never seen without his dhapli, a kind of drum. He would sing beautiful songs with it and also grant blessings and settle disputes by striking his dhapli and listening to its response. There were those in town who believed Dhapli Baba to be crazy; he was kind, gentle, and loving, but also strange and unpredictable.

Once a dispute arose between two women in the village over a baby who was only two weeks old. Each woman claimed the baby was hers. Both of the women were known to have given birth two weeks earlier, but no one could tell who was the true mother.

"Look at his features," said one of the women. "He looks just like me. Obviously I am the real mother."

"Look how he smiles when he hears my voice," said

the second woman. "I am the real mother."

No one could decide, so the village chief brought the two women, the infant, and the crowd that had gathered to Dhapli Baba and asked him to solve this riddle.

"I need only ask my dhapli," said the saint, "and I will soon know the truth." He struck his dhapli three times, then held it up to his ear and closed his eyes. Everyone present fell silent, waiting to see what Dhapli Baba would do.

The saint murmured, then nodded his head. "Yes, yes," he said quietly, "yes, I understand. . . . What? No, no, I don't think that's a good idea. . . no, it isn't possible. . . but. . . yes, I will tell them, but I don't know if they will do it. . . . Very well." The saint opened his eyes and said, "My Dhapli says that both women are correct. The child belongs to both of them. The only fair thing is to divide him between them equally. Bring me a saw, and I will split the baby down the middle."

"No!" cried one of the women. "Give the baby to her. She is the mother and I am the liar. Punish me as you like, just please don't hurt the baby."

"I am sorry," said the saint. "My dhapli has spoken, and I must abide by its wishes. Please bring me a saw."

"No!" cried the woman again.

The village chief stepped in and said, "Enough, Baba. The matter has been settled. The real mother will get the child. There is no need to cut him in two." And saying this, he handed the baby to the second woman, who smiled triumphantly.

"This lady is not the mother," said Dhapli Baba. "The woman who confessed to lying is. As soon as I mentioned cutting the child, she cried out, renounced her claim, and volunteered to be punished so that the child would be saved. This other woman had no such reaction. Only a true mother would relinquish her child to save it."

At this everyone turned to the woman holding the

child. Her smile faded and she, too, burst into tears. "He is right!" she cried. "My child died three days ago and I wanted this other one so badly. But now I see that I was wrong. That lady loves this baby more than I do. Please give him back to her."

The village chief took the baby and returned him to his rightful mother, who dropped to the feet of the saint and started rubbing the bottom of his soles with her forehead. "Bless you, Baba," she said, "for knowing love when you see it." And everyone there was filled with joy to see such happiness.

Nervously Lakshman held the cup in both hands

King Janaka and Lakshman

Once upon a time there was a famous king named Janaka. He was at once a king, a saint, a scholar, and a great teacher. Though he was a wealthy and powerful king, he still maintained his yogic practice with great devotion.

Janaka had four beautiful daughters whom he had married to the four sons of a neighboring king. One day Ram, one of the sons, came to visit with his younger brother Lakshman. The two brothers came to learn the wisdom of the great teacher.

Lakshman was young, and though he had aspirations to become a great yogi himself, he knew little of the world. Upon arriving at the palace, his expectations of King Janaka were dashed. He had looked forward to experiencing the austere life of a monk, a seeker of truth; instead what they found was a stunning palace surrounded by lush fruit trees.

King Janaka greeted them himself, seated on a golden throne.

When Lakshman saw this luxury he asked himself, "Why is this father-in-law of mine, known throughout the land as a sage, an ascetic, living amid the same riches as any other king? How can he consider himself a saint?"

Lakshman had no answer to such questions, and they continued to bother him over the following days, as Janaka entertained the brothers with dancing girls, sumptuous feasts, and games. Soon Lakshman's mind became so distracted by the many pleasures in Janaka's palace that he hardly heard a word the king had to say to him, and he began to wonder if this was the proper way to live after all.

Janaka quickly noticed the situation, and with his enlightened mind he immediately understood what the young man was going through. When Lakshman was alone Janaka approached him and said, "Lakshman, have you seen my palace yet?"

"Indeed I have, Sir," said Lakshman. "It is the most amazing place I have ever seen."

"I would like you to see it again."

Lakshman saw no point in touring the palace again, but he wished to honor any request of the king's, so he agreed.

Janaka handed Lakshman a cup brimming with coconut oil. "Would you please carry this for me while we walk through the palace?"

"Of course, Sir," said Lakshman, though it seemed like a strange request.

"It is extremely important that you do not spill even a single drop of oil. Now follow me."

Nervously Lakshman held the cup in both hands and did his best to follow the king. The oil quivered on the lip of the cup; the slightest jarring and it would spill. The king took him through the royal gardens, around the pool of lotus blossoms, but Lakshman's eyes were fixed on the cup

King Janaka

as his feet carefully felt each step. They crossed the palace kitchen, where the beguiling aromas of cardamom and coriander enveloped them, but Lakshman might as well have been noseless. A troupe of dancing girls passed them. The girls had golden skin and perfumes even more fragrant than the kitchen, but all Lakshman knew was that someone had passed and nearly made him lose his balance.

At last they ended up where they had started. "So, Lakshman," said King Janaka, "What was the most delightful thing you encountered in my palace?"

"To be honest, Sir," said Lakshman, "I was concentrating so hard on the cup of oil that I didn't really notice anything. I am sorry."

"Don't be," said Janaka, smiling. "That is how I live all the time. The cup of oil is always in my palm, and I am always careful not to spill it. The cup is my life, and it is filled to the brim with divine love which I must carry for my Lord, who has entrusted it to me. The cup is all I can afford to dwell on, whether I am in a monastery or a palace."

Then Lakshman's eyes glittered with understanding, and he felt his body fill with love.

The king happily performed the ritual

The Guru and
the King

nce upon a time there was a king. He was a good king and cared for his country and his people very much. Every day he worked long hours settling disputes, watching his country's finances, maintaining his army, making speeches, appointing his ministers, and doing all the other daily tasks that fell to him. He was particularly concerned with making sure that his subjects had enough land on which to live, food to eat, clothes to wear, and work to keep them busy and prosperous. He knew that if he made a wrong decision about which crops to grow or how to defend his kingdom, disaster could strike and bring suffering to vast numbers of his subjects. He came to count his gold almost daily.

Whenever more riches came in through taxes and trading with other kingdoms he felt released, but when he had to spend vast sums to maintain his army and repair his castles he felt that his kingdom was vulnerable and he himself was a failure. Over the years this responsibility made the king exhausted and depressed.

One day he went to his guru, who lived in a hut high in the mountains. The king said, "Respected Guruji, I am deeply troubled by my kingdom. Every time I solve one problem another pops up. I solve that second problem and then there is a third. Every day there are new disputes, new puzzles to solve. I have no time to spend with my wife and son, because I am constantly worried about tomorrow. I have no peace. I am tired and sad. What should I do?"

The guru said, "If being a king is so tiring, leave your kingdom and come live with me in peace."

"But I could never leave my kingdom without a proper ruler!" said the king. "Even with my experience the problems are just barely kept in check. Without a good ruler lawlessness would increase, organization would break down, and my people's lives would grow insecure. I have always been responsible for their well-being."

"Give your kingdom to your son. Then you can come and live with me in peace."

"But my son is only eight years old. He could never rule the kingdom."

"Then give your kingdom to me," said the guru. "I will rule it and look after the interests of your people."

For the first time in years, the king's face brightened. "That would be wonderful! You are the wisest person I know. I am sure you would be an even better ruler than me."

The guru placed a clay pot of water in front of the king. "Then take some water in your hands and purify your body and mind. Say that today, on this first day of Brahma, you donate your kingdom to me, and pour the water into my hands."

The king happily performed the ritual. He poured the

water into the guru's hands, saying, "From now onward I cease to be king. You and only you are king of this country."

The guru drank the water and said, "I accept this gift of God through you and take responsibility for the kingdom into my hands."

Hearing these words, the king felt the weight of responsibility falling off him like water. "All right, Sire," he said. "Allow me to leave."

"What will you do?"

"I will instruct my ministers that you are now king and that your orders must be obeyed. I will then take my wife and son to another country where we will begin a new life, perhaps even start a business."

"That would be foolish," said the guru. "You would find that all your old problems returned."

The king grew quiet. "To be honest, I had not thought about what I would do if I were not king."

"I am sure you will find a position well-suited to your talents. Since you are going back to the palace now, would you convey a message for me?"

"Certainly."

"Would you tell my ministers to begin a search for someone to run the daily affairs of my kingdom for me."

The king was taken aback. "But Sire, won't you be running the daily affairs?"

"Of course not," said the guru. "I am a saint. I cannot go live in the palace. I will rule here from my hut, while my servant implements my orders."

"But Sire," said the king, "you will have to find someone very skilled at running a kingdom. There are very few such people."

"Does that mean you are interested in the job?" asked the guru.

"I am the most qualified," said the king.

"I agree. You know this kingdom far better than I do; I could not find a better servant than you. You may as well live in the palace, since I will not, and you should wear all the clothes of the former king, since they already fit you. But remember: you are no longer the king. You are my servant. The welfare of the kingdom is not your concern; I am responsible for all risks and rewards. You will simply draw a salary from me."

"I accept your proposal," said the king. "I am your servant and will carry out your orders."

"Good. Now go. Your salary will be identical to all your expenses. You will have no savings. Spend what you need on the kingdom—but remember the difference between need and luxury. Avoid luxury, just as your new king does."

"I will do as you have instructed."

"Do not disturb me unnecessarily. Solve every problem on your own that you can. Only come to me when you have a problem."

"I will do my best not to disturb you, Sire," said the king, and he went back to his palace. He announced the changes to the kingdom and went to work as the servant of the guru.

After a month the guru visited the king at the palace. Now that the king was just a servant, he was no longer concerned with appearances. He had dispensed with all luxuries and now lived a frugal life devoted to service. The guru asked him if he was at peace.

"I am, Sire," said the king, "for I have found the perfect calling."

"I noticed that you haven't asked me about anything."

"I have solved everything so far, and I didn't want to disturb you."

"Good. But it seems as though you are working just as hard as before."

"Harder. But now the work feels easy. I work for you,

The guru visited the king at the palace

whom I love deeply, and I am gratified to think that I might be contributing to the welfare of the kingdom in whatever way I can."

"Enjoy your new calling, my son. And remember that I am always mindful of the interests of my kingdom, and that you work for me. I will visit my kingdom again."

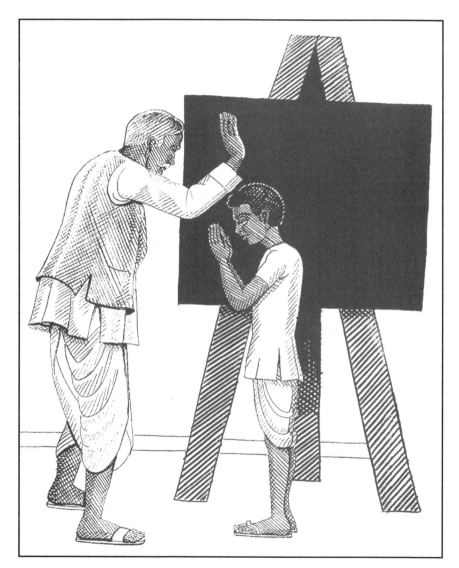

The teacher began to beat the boy

The Lesson

teacher decided to teach his students about anger. "Anger is a fire element," he told them. "It burns the life force, the energy that keeps us alive. It destroys the balance of the body chemistry and makes you forgetful. Your memory becomes weak and your eyes red, and eventually you will become blind. Avoid anger if you want to become a wise person." He stopped talking. "That is enough for today. Write down what I have told you. Tomorrow I will expect each of you to repeat today's lesson. Go home and memorize it."

The next day the teacher asked each of his students to repeat the lesson on anger. Every one repeated the lesson together except for one slow boy sitting in the corner of the first row. The teacher noticed him sitting silently and walked over to him after the others had finished. "Have you not memorized your lesson?" he asked.

"I did not have time," the boy said, looking down at his desk.

"How could you not have time? It was only a few simple sentences."

The boy only stared at his desk.

"I will give you the benefit of the doubt today, but only today. First thing tomorrow morning I expect you to repeat the lesson."

"I will, Sir," said the boy.

The next morning, when the class had assembled, the teacher stood in front of the boy's desk and said, "All right, tell us what you know about anger."

The boy sat quietly.

"Come on, tell us! You have had plenty of time."

"I just cannot quite seem to get it, Sir," said the boy. "I know it is something about anger and body chemistry, but that is all I remember."

"Not good enough!" said the teacher, slamming his hand on the boy's desk. He felt his stomach churn with frustration. "I know you are mocking me. You have one more day to learn this lesson, or you will be severely punished!" He was too agitated to teach, so he dismissed the class for the day.

The next morning the teacher again asked the boy, "Are you ready to recite your lesson on anger?"

The boy looked the teacher in the face and said, "I am sorry. I still can't remember it."

Then you will be punished!" said the teacher, and he began to beat the boy. At first the boy cried, but after a few hits he began to smile. "You shameless idiot!" yelled the teacher. "You should be deeply humiliated, and instead you are smiling!" He began slapping the boy hard on both cheeks.

The boy then began to laugh, and said, "Now I understand! Now I see what anger does to a man. It makes him forgetful and blind. You are beating me, but I am avoiding becoming angry about it."

The teacher stopped slapping the boy and stood there, breathing heavily. "Yes," he said, "I see that you have learned the lesson, but I have not. Forgive me. You have passed the test, and I have failed."

*"Why is it that I work myself to the bone
for only twenty rupees a day?"*

The Difficult Job

n a small town of northern India there was a temple where a saint lived, serving Lord Krishna and caring for the old temple building. For six months a laborer named Ram Prasad had also worked at the temple, restoring the ancient stonework. Every evening Ram watched as the saint took the hundreds of rupees that were donated to him every day and parceled out twenty for Ram. Finally Ram could take this no more and, as he was receiving his wages, said, "Why is it, O saint, that I work myself to the bone for a mere twenty rupees a day, while you do nothing but sit by the fireplace and earn hundreds?"

"A fair question," said the saint. "I'll tell you what. Bring another laborer to restore the temple tomorrow. I have a new job for you that pays twice the wage."

"Thank you, sir!" said Ram, who hurried home after

paying his due respects.

The next day Ram brought another man to do the masonry. He went to the saint and said, "Okay, I am ready to do my new job."

"Very good," said the saint. "What I need you to do is sit here and not make a single movement."

"That's all?" said Ram.

"That's all."

"What could be easier? How long do you need me to do this for?"

"All day."

"All day? For twice my wages? I think I'll like this job very much!" And Ram proceeded to sit in a lotus posture without moving. For the first few minutes as he sat he thought about what he would do with his extra money. Then he tried to figure out what purpose he was serving by sitting still. Then his mind began to wander from subject to subject. The more he tried to stop his thinking and just relax, the faster his mind went. He began thinking about why he was thinking so much, and then thinking about what it meant that he was thinking about thinking. His legs fell asleep and started tingling. Finally he could stand it no more and jumped up, saying, "Enough! How many hours have I been sitting?"

"Perhaps fifteen minutes," said the saint.

"That cannot be!"

The saint said nothing.

"Please, there must be something more useful that I can do."

"Believe me, what you are doing is extremely valuable."

"But my mind makes me crazy when I sit."

"Then you need a focus. Concentrate on your breath and say 'Ram' as you inhale and exhale. This is called japa."

Ram tried this, and it went well for the first few minutes. But again his mind tricked him with random thoughts and he kept having to start over. In an hour he lost his place more than a hundred times. Wrestling with his own mind wore him down, and he began to feel extremely mentally tired. "It is impossible!" he said, rising from his place.

The saint was sitting nearby doing his own japa. Slowly he opened his eyes and said, "What is impossible?"

"To say 'Ram' with each breath. That kind of concentration cannot be achieved."

"Nothing is impossible. You see me sitting here doing it with you. So far you have worked for an hour and a half. You have another six and a half hours to finish your day. Please sit down and continue."

"No, please! Six and a half hours and I will lose my mind! Give me something elsc to do."

"The only other job is that of laborer, as you see that man doing over there. But as you know, it only pays half as much as your present position."

"I will take it!" said Ram. "Anything but this."

"All right then," said the saint. "Now you see that keeping busy may be hard for the body, but it is very easy for the mind. You thought I was doing nothing sitting all day, but now you understand how difficult the job of a saint is."

"I understand all too well, sir," said Ram, "and I pay tribute to you. Never will I underestimate your skills again. Now please let me go or I shall go crazy."

"You are free to leave," said the saint, and Ram hurried off, defeated by his mind. The saint watched him go, then returned to his soothing japa.

He grabbed a fat mango and scampered
back to the forest with it

The Monkeys and
the Mango Tree

nce upon a time there was a beautiful
mango orchard, laden with ripe fruit. A
band of monkeys passing from tree to
tree saw the mangos and entered the
orchard, where they began tearing into
as many mangos as they could reach,
dropping one after a few bites to go impatiently on to the
next. Suddenly one of the monkeys screamed as he was hit
by a large stone. They all turned to see the orchard keeper
and his assistants hurling stones at them. The monkeys ran
off to the safety of the nearby forest, returning as soon as
the men left. But no sooner did they begin eating mangos
again than a hail of stones greeted them, and again they had
to retreat. This pattern went on throughout the day, until
most of the monkeys had sustained injuries.

The chief of the monkeys called a meeting. "Enough of
this!" he said. "We come from the noble lineage of the

monkey-god Hanuman, faithful servant of Rama, but getting battered for the sake of some fruit does not feel noble to me. What can we do?"

The cleverest of the monkeys spoke up. "What we need is a mango tree of our own. Then we could eat all the fruit in peace. I have heard that mango trees come from the seed inside the fruit. Humans put the seed in the ground, and then a mango tree comes out. We can steal a fruit, put the seed in the ground, and make our own tree."

All the monkeys thought this was an excellent idea, so they sent a young, quick monkey back into the orchard. He dodged several stones from the orchard keeper, grabbed a fat mango, and scampered back to the forest with it. There, the monkeys dug a hole, put the seed inside, and covered it up. Then they all sat expectantly, watching the spot, waiting for the tree.

After ten minutes there was no tree, and some of the younger monkeys grew restless and wandered off. Then some of the older monkeys began to wander off too, until the chief said, "Get back here! Where do you think you're going?"

"We can't wait any more. There are all those mangos over there ready to be eaten."

They all sat expectantly, watching the spot

"Don't you understand? We'll get nowhere doing that. We need to wait for our own tree. I'm sure it will come soon."

So the monkeys waited an entire day, but nothing happened.

A second full day passed, and still nothing happened.

"It isn't natural to wait this long for anything!" said one of the monkeys. "Let's dig it up and see what's wrong."

"Patience," said the chief.

A third day passed, and nothing happened. All the monkeys begged the chief to let them dig up the seed to see what was happening. Eventually, he agreed.

The dug down, uncovered the seed, and broke off the tiny sprout, which had just begun to germinate.

"You see, my children!" said the chief. "Wishes do not come true overnight. Alas, we monkeys were not meant to be gardeners. We had the dream of a tree, and the seed of one, but not what it takes to get from one to the other."

And the band of monkeys wandered off, reaching for the closest fruit at hand.

The old servant opened the door
and recognized the saint at once

The Merchant Who Would Not Go to Heaven

nce upon a time there lived a merchant named Lala who was well known for his charity. Whenever a saint passed through town the merchant would provide him with food, clothes, money, and anything else the saint would accept. One day, a highly realized saint came to town. He was warmly greeted by the merchant and taken home with him, where he was served delicious food and given a room for the evening.

The saint was very pleased by the merchant, and before he went to sleep he said to him, "Lala, your deeds have earned you a place in Heaven."

"Thank you for saying so, Maharaj," said Lala. "Perhaps one day I will be ready."

"That day is today," said the saint. "I can take you to Heaven right now."

Lala looked pained. "Oh, that is what I desire more than anything, but I am afraid it is impossible."

"But why?"

"As you can see, I have no wife. She died years ago. My son is only ten years old and needs my care. It will be some time before he is old enough to take over my business, but then I would gladly take you up on your offer."

"How long until you are ready?"

Lala thought for a while, then said, "In fifteen years he will be twenty-five and capable of running the business. Then I can go."

"Fifteen years it shall be," said the saint. "I will return then and fulfill my promise."

Fifteen years to the day after their first meeting, the saint returned to the merchant's home. A watchdog lying by the front door with a litter of puppies wagged her tail at him as he knocked. Lala's old servant opened the door and recognized the saint at once.

"Welcome, sir!" said the servant. "It has been a long time. I am afraid my old master is no longer here. His son now runs the business."

"Where is Lala?"

"He died of a heart attack five years ago. But please, sir, this house is as it was before; the door is always open for saints. Come in and have a warm meal."

The saint entered the house, and the dogs came with them, too. As the saint sat waiting he thought how sad it was that he had not been able to take Lala to Heaven. He closed his eyes to meditate, and suddenly through his yogic vision he realized that Lala was reincarnated as the female dog beside him. "Lala!" he said. "What are you doing there?"

"I died of a heart attack when my son was only twenty," said Lala. "At the time his new wife was pregnant, and though he was successfully running the business I worried

A watchdog lay by the front door with her litter of puppies

that there was no one to protect the house and his family, so I preferred to come back as a dog."

"I understand," said the saint. "Are you ready to come with me now?"

The dog sighed. "Thank you very much for returning to honor your promise. I would love that more than anything, but I am afraid that I cannot go. These puppies depend on me for everything. In two years they will be grown and will be able to defend the house. Then I will be free."

"Very well," said the saint. "I will return in two years."

Two years later the saint returned to the house. Three children—one seven, one five, and one three—were playing with several dogs and with a parrot in a cage. The house seemed very lively and happy. The saint searched in vain for the dog that was Lala. When the old servant greeted him, the saint asked, "What became of the mother of these dogs?"

"She was killed fighting off thieves a year ago, sir," said the servant. "You would not have believed how she fought before dying. Please come in and take some food from us." The servant shooed the dogs and children away from the saint and left to put together a bowl of food.

As soon as they were alone the parrot said, "Squawk! Welcome back. Squawk! Welcome back."

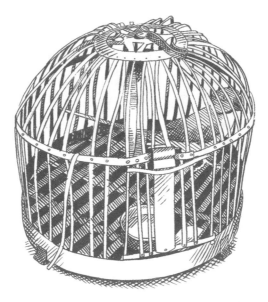

Squawk! Welcome back!"

The saint meditated and used his yogic vision to confirm that Lala had been reincarnated as the parrot. "Hello, Lala," he said. "Now you have no burdens. Your house is protected and your family is well off. It is time to go to Heaven." He opened the cage and reached toward the parrot.

"Please don't take me!" said Lala. "I am just fine here. My son and daughter-in-law are quite fond of me and would really miss me. My grandsons and granddaughter love to talk with me and to feed me by hand. Thank you very much for remembering your promise but I have no desire to leave this world and go to heaven. What would I do with no attachments or responsibilities? This cage is my heaven. I'm sorry to have made you come all this way, but I have learned my lesson and no longer desire anything I do not have."

The saint was astonished, but he abided by Lala's wishes, and never again returned to the merchant who had no time for Heaven.

He began passing out whole oranges

The Saint Who Could Do Miracles

here once was a saint named Lahiri Baba who prayed every night to be granted the ability to work miracles for the needy. One night the saint was invited to dinner at a friend's house.

The friend's brother, who was an atheist, also came to dinner. The brother brought six oranges to give to the host's six children, but out of deference to the saint he gave them to Lahiri Baba to distribute instead.

Lahiri Baba immediately went outside and called to the children who were playing in the nearby lane, "Come quickly and I will give you an orange." The children came running, but not before they had called their friends, and those friends had called their friends, and soon there were fifty children in the house begging for oranges.

The atheist watched all this and said, "Look what you have done now, Lahiri Baba. These children were promised a whole orange, and now you can only give them a tiny wedge each."

"I have faith that my promise will be fulfilled," said the saint, and he began passing out whole oranges.

The children crowded around Lahiri Baba until the atheist could no longer see the saint, only the occasional child squirming out of the pack with an orange clenched tightly to his or her chest. As the atheist kept watching, more and more children ran off with oranges, until all fifty children were gone. Lahiri Baba was left alone with the same six oranges he had held at first.

"How did you do that?" asked the atheist. "That is not possible."

"All things are possible if you have faith and your intentions are true," said the saint.

Over the following months Lahiri Baba became well known as a miracle worker. He would sit in the town square and produce food for the hungry and gold coins for those who had nothing. The atheist witnessed some of these things with his own eyes but was always skeptical. If miracles are possible, he thought to himself, why are they so rare. Why doesn't every saint work miracles for everyone who needs one?

The next time the atheist saw Lahiri Baba, the saint was in the hospital with broken arms and legs. "What happened, Lahiri Baba?" asked the atheist.

"I have learned my lesson," said the saint. "I let the whole town watch me do miracles for the needy. Then one evening as I was walking home some thieves grabbed me from behind and said, 'Saint, make some gold for us right now or we will break your bones.'

"'I cannot,' I said, 'I can only do miracles for those in need. You are not needy.'

"But they did not believe me and broke my arms and legs. It is the price I paid for doing miracles in public. You can never make everyone happy, and every person you help makes someone else envious. My ego delighted in the gratitude and amazement people showed me, and I earned bad karma for it. It is much better to ignore such powers and spend more time in prayer instead. I thank God for teaching me the lesson I deserved."

Two friends went to hear the discourse of a saint

Saraswati Nadi

nce a middle class man from Northern India and his friend went to hear the discourse of a saint. The saint, a yogi who was an expert in the hidden power of the human body, told them, "You should always abstain from harsh language, cursing others, and telling lies, because for one brief moment every day the subtle nerve called Saraswati nadi, which originates in the first chakra and terminates in the tongue, becomes active and whatever you speak at that moment comes true. Whenever that happens people say that Saraswati, the goddess of speech, was sitting on their tongue.

"By speaking truthfully and kindly," the yogi went on, "you nourish the Saraswati nadi with life-giving divine nectar, but harsh words produce toxins that spoil the divine nectar. If you want to have your wishes fulfilled, you should practice speaking only truth for a fortnight during an ascending moon cycle and fast on the day before the full moon. Then, on the full moon, stay awake all night and repeat the wish like a mantra. The wish will be fulfilled when both nostrils operate together and energy flows freely through another subtle nerve called Sushumna nadi.

"Practice this," said the yogi, "and when your wish comes true, think about what could be accomplished if you abstained from harsh words and lies for your entire life." The Yogi ended his discourse with a chant.

As the man and his friend returned home, the man was very excited. "Did you follow all that the saint said?" he asked his friend. "When shall we begin the discipline?"

"Surely you don't believe all that?" said his friend. "There is no such thing as miracles. Wishes don't come true."

"I have faith," said the man. "At least accompany me when I try."

For the next two weeks the man spoke only pleasant, truthful words. He fasted the day of the full moon, sitting in his house with a brick before him. That evening his friend came over and sat beside him while the man stared at the brick, chanting, "Become gold!" through the night. Hour after hour he chanted, fighting off sleep, and hour after hour nothing happened. Around dawn anger and disgust overpowered him. Doubt, the greatest enemy of spiritual progress, took hold in his mind. Impatient and exhausted, he shouted, "Become a heap of ashes then, if not gold!"

At that moment the brick transformed into a heap of ashes. The man clapped his hand over his mouth. "O goddess Saraswati," he said, "what have I done? I missed you when you were on my tongue!"

The man slumped in despair, but his friend leaped to his feet and began dancing in ecstasy. "Your failure has awakened my faith!" he said. "I shall be rich on the next full moon!"

The king offered Vashishtha flowers and fruits

The Wish-Fulfilling Cow

nce upon a time there lived a king named Vishwamitra who ruled northern India. The king had just defeated his enemies in a great battle and now had almost unlimited power. As he led his army back from the battle, they happened to pass the forest where lived Vashishtha—the saint who had taught seven generations of the king's family. The king had never been to the saint's home, so he decided to pay homage in person and tell him the news of the great victory. The entire army camped in the forest and the next morning, after bathing in a nearby stream, the king visited Vashishtha.

Vashishtha was very pleased to see Vishwamitra, whom he had taught since childhood but had not seen since he had become king. The king offered Vashishtha flowers and fruits and then told him of his decisive victory. After that he asked the saint to grant him leave so that he and his army could return to their kingdom.

"O king," said Vashishtha, "you and your army are exhausted and starving from long days of battle. It is the least I can do to serve you a good meal before you continue on your journey."

"Respected Sir," replied the king, "it would be impossible for you to feed my army of ten thousand. Thank you for your kind offer, but if you will excuse us we will return to our city."

"It is said that if a guest goes hungry at a house then all the householder's good deeds are for naught. Fear not, my king; I will feed your army with pleasure and without difficulty. Please accept my hospitality and return to your city tomorrow morning."

The king did not wish to offend his spiritual teacher, so he said, "If you insist, Sir, we would be honored to dine at your hermitage this evening."

The king returned to his army and gave the word for every man to wash himself and prepare to dine at the hermitage. The king's generals gathered and questioned him as to how he could ever have agreed to such a plan. Where would the poor hermit find food for ten thousand? Who would cook it? With what pots? The evening would be a disaster and the old man would be humiliated.

The king was equally worried. He knew it was impossible, but he had been unable to refuse his old teacher. In the afternoon he sent twenty men with pots to offer their services in gathering firewood, chopping vegetables, or whatever else Vashishtha might need. But the men soon returned and one of them relayed a message to the king: "Shri Vashishtha says to thank you for your kind offer, but he needs no help. Dinner will be served one hour before sunset. Please arrive then."

"What could he possibly be serving?" said the king. "Did

Divine beings flew out of the ears of the cow

the preparations seem to be going well?"

"As far as we could tell, my lord, there have been no preparations of any kind."

This made the king even more upset. Perhaps his old teacher had lost touch with reality. He worried about the evening until it was time to march his army to the hermitage, but there was nothing to be done. As soon as the evening sun started to go down, he led his army through the forest until they reached the tiny cottage. There was no sign of any feast at all, just one cow tethered to a tree nearby.

Vashishtha came out of his cottage and greeted the king, his generals, and his men with a smile on his face. "Thank you so much for coming," he said. Then he walked over to the cow and placed his hand on her back. "Mother Kamadhenu, King Vishwamitra has come for dinner to our humble cottage. Please arrange a suitable feast for him and his men."

As the army watched in amazement, a host of divine beings flew out of the ears of the cow and within a very short time had washed the hands of every man and placed a clean mat at his feet. At a sign from the king the men all sat on their mats.

Vashishtha said, "Thank you all for coming. You will each be served whatever you would like—please eat as much as you want, as there is an unending supply of everything." Then he turned to the cow and said, "Mother Kamadhenu, I have promised each man his choicest food. Please provide them with it."

From the ears of the cow came uncountable divine beings, each carrying a plate covered by lotus leaves. When a plate had been placed in front of each man they removed the leaves and each found the exact food he desired the most. After offering amazed prayers and thanks, each man reached for the good things at hand. The food was indescribably delicious, and no matter how much they ate their plates always remained full.

After all had put aside desire for food and drink, more divine beings emerged from the ears of the miraculous cow bearing water to clean each man's hands and face. Everyone was awed by the feast. The king, who had been in a strange daze since the first appearance of the divine beings, leaned close to the ear of the saint and said, "Respected sir, this has been an unforgettable evening. Now please give us leave to return to our camp and care for our horses and elephants."

"They have already been given everything they require," said Vashishtha. "They are my guests as well. But do return to your camp; you are exhausted and have much to think about."

That night the king could not sleep at all. The cow, Kamadhenu, dominated his mind. I am one of the most powerful men on earth, he thought, yet I could not do what that cow did this evening. The king's tremendous victory over the neighboring kingdoms, which only a day before had filled him with pride, suddenly seemed insignificant. He had the power of life and death over thousands of people, but he could not fulfill their desires. Without that cow I am nothing, he thought.

In the morning he called his most trusted general to him and said, "Please go to Vashishtha and tell him that his cow is too valuable to be kept unguarded in the forest. For its own protection only the king should possess it."

The general went to the hermitage and delivered the message. Vashishtha was stunned. "Please tell the king that he has all the riches in the world and does not need this cow. Kamadhenu is all I have; my entire life depends on her. Moreover, she is a very special cow that only a saint is entitled to. Please tell the king he cannot have something that he has not earned."

All this time the king had been waiting, planning out in his head all the things he would do as soon as he possessed Kamadhenu. When he saw the general return empty-handed he flew into a rage. "How dare you return without that cow! What is your excuse?"

The general relayed the saint's message, which only made the king more furious. "If anyone is entitled to that cow it is me! Gather some of your men and go take that cow at once."

The general and four of his officers went to the hermitage. Vashishtha was standing out front and watched sadly as the general walked up to the cow and with his sword cut the rope that tied her to the tree. The cow did not want to be moved and fought as they tried to lead her away, but they pricked the back of her legs with their swords. She mooed, and the saint said, "Mother Kamadhenu, save yourself from this torture." At these words divine beings bearing spears flew out of the ears of the cow and drove the general and his officers back to their camp.

When the king saw this he cried and screamed at the same time. "I cannot go on without that cow! Prepare the entire army for battle!"

"I would not recommend it, my lord," said the general. "Why don't we just return to our kingdom? You are the ruler of half of India. Isn't that enough?"

"Not nearly enough. Prepare for battle."

Vashishtha knew that when man becomes obsessed with desire he loses his reason. He knew the king had seen a glimpse of something he could not live without, so he told his cow to protect herself when the time came.

As soon as the king and his army drew near the hermitage a divine army flew from the ears of the cow and routed them. Soon the king and his generals were brought as captives before the saint. "Now, Sir," said the chieftain of the divine army, "what punishment is strong enough for this arrogant king whose family you have served for seven generations?"

"His own tortured thought is punishment enough," said the saint. "Please let him go."

As soon as the king was released he fell at the feet of the saint and began to cry. "Forgive me, kind Vashishtha," he said. "You were so generous to me and I have repaid you with betrayal. I now know that I cannot live without this cow. What can I ever do to attain her?"

"Everyone is entitled to this cow," said the saint, "but one cannot have this cow and worldly possessions at the same time. You must divest yourself of all you own, for material goods only feed one's pride, not one's wisdom. This cow flees from pride and egotism. Once you have reached a stage of spiritual development where you are no

*Soon the king and his generals were brought
as captives before the saint*

longer subject to the world of illusion, where you have will-
ful control over your own mind and can withdraw from
mental distractions and enter a state of bliss, then
Kamadhenu will come to you of her own accord. Any wish
will be fulfilled, though you will desire little. But you must
decide which you want most—the material kingdom, or
Kamadhenu."

"Kamadhenu," sobbed the king, "Kamadhenu alone."

Vishwamitra returned to his kingdom. Festivals were
held to commemorate his historic victory and the entire city
celebrated for days, but for the king the world had lost its
color and food had lost its taste. As soon as the city had settled into a normal routine he renounced his kingdom,
appointed a wise minister to take his place, and became an
ascetic. Kings are slaves to their kingdom—he had glimpsed
freedom.

Never in his life had the priest heard this sound

The Watchman

nce upon a time, in the temple of Krishna in Vrindaban, there was a night watchman who guarded the temple from thieves, for in the inner shrine was a statue of Krishna with a large diamond imbedded in the crown. All night to keep himself awake he would sing devotional songs known as bhajans. One night the chief priest, who was a renowned classical musician, was walking by the temple and heard the strident, off-key songs escaping from within. He grew angry and burst into the temple.

"Stop that racket!" shouted the priest. "Your harsh voice disturbs the serenity of the temple. Don't you know Lord Krishna is taking his rest at this time? Get out of this temple and never return!"

The shocked watchman left at once, and after a few minutes the priest's anger subsided. He realized he had been impetuous, for now there was no one but himself to guard the temple. He decided to stay the night and look for a new watchman the next morning.

Hardly an hour had passed when the priest heard heavy footsteps coming from the inner shrine of the temple. He checked both doors to the shrine, but they were still locked. No one could have slipped past him. He put his ear up to the door. The footsteps continued. Fearing that some clever thief had somehow found another way into the shrine, the priest unlocked the door and rushed in. To his astonishment he found the statue of Krishna pacing back and forth.

O blessed night, thought the priest. Because of all my good work Lord Krishna has come to honor me in person. "My Lord!" cried the priest, falling to his knees. "To what do I owe this honor?"

"I cannot sleep," replied Krishna angrily. "The man who sings me lullabies all night is missing."

The priest was stunned for a moment but then recovered his wits and said, "I will sing for you, my Lord. I am a most accomplished musician." The priest got his tambura from the next room, tuned it, and began to sing in classical ragas the same bhajan he had heard the watchman sing. He played perfectly, his voice hitting each note with precision.

After listening for several minutes Krishna waved his hand and said, "I have heard classical ragas for centuries and could sing them myself much better than you. No, I must have the singing of that watchman. For fifteen years I have listened to it and now it is the only thing that soothes me."

"But my Lord," said the priest, "he is tone-deaf and has a nasal voice. Allow me to play my tambura while you relax to its musical drone."

"Don't bore me!" said Krishna. "Get the watchman at once."

The frightened priest could not argue further and rushed to the house of the watchman. He heard sobbing coming from within, and knocked on the door. After several moments the watchman answered, tears rolling down his face.

"What are you crying for?" asked the priest.

"I have been separated from my beloved temple," said the watchman. "My life is only worth living in devotion to my Lord."

"Then you are in luck," said the priest bitterly. "Lord Krishna has come to life in the shrine and he is asking for you to come sing to him."

Now it was tears of joy that flowed from the eyes of the watchman. He followed the priest at once. When they reached the temple Krishna was still inside pacing.

"I could not sleep after you left," said Krishna. "Please, start your bhajans, and lock the door as you have done every night."

The priest locked the door. The watchman had fallen to his knees and was gazing at Krishna in wonderment. The priest had to shake him, and then the watchman began to sing, tears still rolling down his cheeks. It was as harsh as ever, and even more faltering, and the priest winced, expecting Krishna to strike them both for insulting him with such noise. But he looked at Krishna, and the god had a look of deep contentment on his face. Then the priest heard a sound in the watchman's voice that had been there all along, but that he had never noticed. It was as if he had been watching the reflection on the surface of a lake, and then suddenly by shifting his eyes he saw for the first time the pure depths beneath.

The priest had performed concerts all over India, and had listened to many more, but never in his life had he heard this sound. It rose in his body like a crystal bell, and he understood that everything he had heard before then was just notes, just sound, and that what he was hearing now was pure love. For the first time in his life he experienced bliss.

The god had a look of deep contentment

The night passed slowly. As the watchman sang the statue of Krishna returned to its pedestal and resumed its usual position. When the eastern sky began to turn red the watchman stopped singing and prostrated himself on the ground before the statue, tears of joy still falling.

For a long time the priest waited for the watchman to rise. Finally, when he began to worry that the morning worshippers would start to arrive, he walked over to the watchman and said, "You can get up now. Your duty is done. Go home and sleep." But the watchman did not respond. The priest gently shook him, and the watchman's body rolled over. His soul had risen to be with his Lord, and though he was dead his face glowed with bliss, his body shone like the morning sun, and the temple shrine was filled with light.

The woman was transformed into a sow
with loaves of bread stuck to her snout

God Helps
Those Who
Help Themselves

 ne day Shakti, the Divine Mother, asked Shiva to leave their abode on Mount Kailash and go with her to the world to see how all their children fared. Shiva summoned Nandi, his sacred bull, and asked him to take them around the world through the sky-path.

As they were traveling, Shakti heard someone chanting "Aum Namah Shivaye," her favorite mantra. She saw a poor man sitting on the ground repeating the mantra. Beside him were his starving wife and son. As Shakti watched, the son begged his mother for something to eat. "I have nothing but love, my son, to give you," the woman said, and tears began falling from her eyes.

Shakti could not bear this sight, and said to Shiva, "They are your devotees, my Lord; can you not do something to help them?"

Shiva and Shakti

"That family quarrels constantly with each other," said Shiva. "They are not ready to be helped."

"But you are omnipotent!" said Shakti. "You could save them if you wanted."

"On Earth, all beings are bound by the law of karma. Everyone gets what they are destined to get; no one gets what he does not deserve."

"But if you can help them, you should."

Shiva shrugged. "I will try." He disappeared from the back of Nandi and reappeared beside the poor family. "Open your eyes, my dear devotee," he said to the man. "I am Shiva. I am pleased that you chant my wife's favorite mantra. You may ask me for any boon."

The man opened his eyes and his mouth dropped open as well. He stared in terror at the god before him and struggled to speak. Finally he managed to say, "I am paralyzed by your presence, my Lord. Please grant my wife the boon instead."

"There are enough boons to go around," said Shiva. "I will grant one to her and to your son as well. Now please, simply ask for what you desire."

"I, I, I cannot think," stammered the man. "Please ask my wife first."

"Very well," said Shiva, turning to the woman. "Dear lady, ask me for a boon. Your husband's devotion has pleased me."

The woman did not hesitate. "My son is starving, my Lord. The only thing I wish is bread. Please grant to me a cart full of fresh loaves."

"So be it," said Shiva. Instantly a cartload of breads appeared before them.

Seeing the cart piled with bread, the husband lost his reluctance to speak. "How foolish you are, woman!" he screamed at his wife. "These breads will mold before we can eat one tenth of them. Once in a lifetime does Shiva grant anyone a boon, and you waste yours on bread! Shiva, I know exactly what I want. I want you to turn this woman into a pig, because that is what she is. Turn her into a pig, and let all these breads stick to her nose!"

"As you wish," said Shiva. Before any of them could blink, the woman was transformed into a great pink sow, with loaves of bread stuck to her snout.

The little boy began to cry. "What have you done to my mother?" he sobbed. "I want her back as she was before, without those awful breads."

"So you shall have it," said Shiva. The next moment the woman was back before them, empty-handed. The man and woman looked forlornly at Shiva, knowing that their chance was gone.

"You were granted three boons," said Shiva, "and you are right back where you started." He disappeared and returned to the back of Nandi. "You see, my dear," he said to Shakti. "I granted them three boons and it still did not change their fate."

"How sad," said Shakti. "It is true that one must be ready for one's destiny. Let us move away from here."

Who stands here?

They had not traveled far when Shakti again heard someone chanting, "Aum Namah Shivaye." She looked down and
saw a blind beggar sitting on the ground chanting the
mantra. "Another poor soul," she said. "And equally devoted.
Do you think you can help him?"

"I will try," said Shiva. He left Nandi and stood beside
the blind beggar.

Sensing someone near him, the beggar stopped chanting
and asked, "Who stands here?"

"It is Shiva. I am pleased with you and you may ask me
for one boon."

The beggar was silent for a very long time, but Shiva sensed that he was calm, unlike the first man. At long last the beggar said, "If you really are Shiva, please grant my wish that I might see my great grandson eating sweets from a silver plate with a silver spoon."

Shiva smiled. "It is really too much, O blind man, but because you are so wise and careful, I will grant it." And he disappeared.

And fifty years from that moment it came to pass, after the man had led a joyful life that included the magical return of his eyesight, his falling in love with a woman who married him and bore his children, the marriages of those children, the birth of his grandchildren, their marriages and families, and through it all the great wealth that seemed to almost fall out of the sky upon the man and his descendents.

The demon watched the shimmering body of Shakti

Shiva and the Demon

Once upon a time there was a demon who wished to become as powerful as a god. So strong was his wish that he went to Shiva's home and prayed outside it to Shiva day and night for many years.

Shiva was so impressed by the devotion of this demon that he opened his eyes from samadhi—deep meditation on the nature of existence—and came outside. "Demon," he said, "I am pleased with the fervor of your worship. Your faith in me, and the discipline you have practiced, are worthy of reward. Ask for any boon and I shall grant it."

The demon thought for some time about what he should ask for. At last he said, "Lord, if you are pleased with my penance, then grant me the boon that when I place my right palm on top of the head of another, he will be burned to ashes."

"That is a very powerful request," said Shiva, "but you have earned it. The boon is granted." And he closed his eyes, wishing to return to samadhi.

"Allow me to test my new power," said the demon, and he raised his right palm toward Shiva's head.

Shiva jumped back just in time and said, "What are you doing? You must not be so impulsive with the power I have given you. You would have burned me to ashes!"

"Yes I would have," said the demon, smiling, "And then your beautiful wife Shakti would have been all mine!" And he reached for Shiva's head again.

Shiva ran off into the thick forest with the demon right behind him. Shakti, watching from her home, saw her husband being chased by the demon and called to Vishnu, the Lord of Preservation.

Vishnu came to her and said, "What is it you need, great mother?"

"Shiva granted that demon the ability to turn people to ashes with his palm, and now the demon is trying to use it on him so that he can have me. Please help!"

"Very well," said Vishnu. He immediately assumed the form of Shakti and went into the forest. As the demon was chasing Shiva Vishnu stepped out from behind a bush and said, "Where are you going, demon?"

"I am chasing your husband," said the demon.

"What for? It is me you want. And I will happily marry you right now, because you are so handsome and clever. Let that old ascetic be. All he wants is to sit in Samadhi, anyway. He has no attachment to worldly things."

Hearing these words from Shakti was a dream come true for the demon. "Let us get married right now," he said. "Then I will truly have everything a god has."

"So be it," said Vishnu. "But I must have dancing at the wedding. That is how Shiva first won me over; he is the most wonderful dancer in the world, and I love to dance with him."

The demon grew sullen. "I have never learned to dance."

"Don't worry. I will teach you. Few can say that they learned to dance from Shakti herself."

"Yes, please do!" said the demon. "Then I will be as great a dancer as Shiva. Teach me right now, I cannot wait."

"Very well," said Vishnu. His hips began to sway back and forth, and he raised his fingers in a "V" and swept them over his eyes.

The demon watched the shimmering body of Shakti, watched her veils as they rose and fell, and grew very excited. "You are the most beautiful thing in the universe," he said, "and soon you will be all mine."

"You must imitate everything I do," said Vishnu, "if you are to learn the dance."

The demon copied Vishnu as he raised his hands into the air, head rocking from side to side. "Am I as good a dancer as Shiva?" he asked.

"Not yet, but you are getting close. You must go faster." Vishnu sped up the dance, with the demon following him. "Shiva is so fine a dancer," said Vishnu, "that he can anticipate my every move, and each of his gestures mirrors mine exactly."

"Then I, too, can do that," said the demon, copying Vishnu as quickly as he could.

"Oh, my," said Vishnu, "you are a very fine dancer indeed. Never have I seen your equal."

Hearing this praise, the demon went even faster. "I am the greatest dancer," he said. "I can do every gesture at the same instant as you."

"Very good," said Vishnu, and he placed his palm on top of his head. The demon instantly did the same. With a burst of smoke he burned to ashes.

As soon as the demon had burned, Vishnu assumed his real form. Shiva, who had been watching from the safety of

Shiva came out and thanked Vishnu

some nearby bushes, came out and thanked him.

"You are welcome," said Vishnu. "In the future, please be more careful about granting boons to demons with such evil intentions."

"I will," said Shiva, "but they do not worry me. So long as they remain driven by vanity and sensual pleasure, their power will only destroy them." And he closed his eyes and returned to blessed samadhi.

"A hungry saint visited our town"

Narada and the Crazy Saint

nce upon a time the sage Narada was passing through a town and stopped to buy some supplies from a merchant. The merchant seemed very friendly and they began a conversation. Soon Narada was invited to have supper with the merchant and his wife. Narada accepted happily and accompanied the merchant to his house.

They had a wonderful meal, but Narada noticed that he became sad after eating the food cooked by the merchant's wife. After they had finished, Narada asked the merchant, "Why is your wife sad?"

"How did you know that?" asked the startled merchant.

"Because normally after eating such delicious food I feel great joy. But I can feel a sadness in this food."

The merchant and his wife exchanged glances. "You truly are a great sage," said the merchant. "You are right;

we are both sad. We have been unable to have children. We have tried everything—doctors, tantrikas, astrologers, even saints—but nothing seems to work."

"Do you have your horoscopes?" asked Narada.

"Yes," said the merchant, who brought out two horoscopes done by a great astrologer and handed them to Narada. "You are the most learned scholar of this science. Won't you please figure out a way for us to have a child?"

Narada studied the horoscopes. Then he studied the palms of the two. "I am sorry," he said at last. "It seems that you are not destined to have any children." He thanked the couple for the meal and left the house, feeling very sad.

Narada went to Vaikuntha, the abode of Lord Vishnu, and said to Vishnu, "Lord, I have just visited a couple who are very kind and who follow their dharma most sincerely, yet they cannot beget a child. Is there no way to change this?"

Vishnu looked down on Narada and said, "Narada, you know as well as I do that there is no changing the law of karma. What is, is. Everyone gets what they deserve. Life is a series of countless incarnations, and just because one is good in this life does not mean one shall be rewarded in it, or that one was good in a previous life. I cannot interfere in this matter."

Narada left Vaikuntha, still sad. One day years later he was passing through the same town and sought out the merchant. The merchant seemed very happy and invited Narada to supper once again. Narada accepted, though he expected it would be a sad occasion.

When he arrived at the house Narada saw three beautiful children playing outside. "Whose children are these?" he asked.

"Ours," beamed the merchant.

"Yours?"

"Yes. Soon after you left our house a hungry saint visited

"Whose children are these?"

our town and announced, 'Whosoever gives this hungry man one loaf of bread will get one child, two loaves will get two children, and three loaves will get three children.' My wife and I heard him, and though we knew it was not out destiny to have children, we took pity on him, brought him back to our house, and gave him bread. He ate three loaves and said, 'I bless you to have three beautiful children.' We thought he was just a crazy saint, but you can see what happened."

Narada finished another delectable meal with the merchant and his wife, blessed their children, and took his leave. He was very happy for them, but also very confused. He went to Vaikuntha once again and said to Vishnu, "Lord, I have just visited with the unfortunate merchant and his wife, whom you told me were not destined to have children—"

"And they have three," said Vishnu.

"But their horoscopes and their palms. . ."

"It makes no difference. He was blessed by a devoted bhakta of mine. Bhaktas alone can change one's destiny. If they promise something to someone I have to grant it."

"But why?"

"I will answer your question momentarily. But your mind is too agitated to absorb any wisdom now. Let us take a walk while you calm yourself."

Narada and Vishnu took a walk near a village. It was sunset and people were offering their evening prayers. In a nearby temple bells were ringing and a mantra was being chanted. Narada waited for his mind to calm, but he still dwelled on why a bhakta had powers that he himself did not.

Suddenly Vishnu cried out in pain and slumped to the ground, holding his side.

"What is wrong, my lord?" shouted Narada.

"My liver is ruined! Some devotees of mine offered me sweets cooked in rancid oil. I need someone to give me their liver as soon as possible!"

"Yes, my lord," said Narada, and he ran to the temple. "Is there someone who will donate his liver to Lord Vishnu?" Narada shouted. "He is sick and may die without one." But everyone in the temple laughed at him. "I am not crazy! I am Narada; you must have heard of my name." But everyone thought he was crazy and they continued ringing bells and chanting mantras.

Narada ran to a group of beggars gathered near a creek and asked if any would donate their liver to Vishnu. Again no one would. "Try him," they said, pointing at a beggar who was standing in the creek on one leg, chanting a mantra with his eyes closed. "He's the only one crazy enough to do something like that."

Narada waded into the creek and asked the crazy-looking beggar, "Brother, Lord Vishnu is sick and needs a liver immediately. Will you donate yours?"

Suddenly Vishnu slumped to the ground, holding his side

The beggar stopped chanting and opened his eyes. "Of course," he said. "Come to my hut." He lowered his other leg and began walking. Narada followed him to his hut. There the man picked up a knife and sat down in the lotus posture. He meditated for a while and then, taking a deep breath, he stabbed the knife into his side and cut a large opening. Blood flowed down over his legs. He sawed in a circle, with no expression on his face, and then he removed his liver and handed it to Narada. "I hope this helps Lord Vishnu," said the beggar, who then closed his eyes and went into a trance, blood pouring out of his side.

Narada rushed back to Vishnu with the fresh, bleeding liver. When he got there Vishnu was sitting comfortably in a lotus posture.

"Here, my lord," said Narada, "a fresh liver!"

"Where did you find it?" asked Vishnu.

"A crazy beggar gave it to me. Everyone else ignored me."

"Why did you run to so many people when you yourself had one to offer so close at hand?"

Narada stopped short. He had nothing to say.

"Do you think that your life is more important than mine?"

"Certainly not, my lord. I—"

"Perhaps you forgot that you had a liver?"

"Of course not, my lord. It simply . . . never occurred to me."

"Sacrificing your own life was the farthest thing from your mind."

Narada lowered his head. "You are right, my lord. I am sorry."

Vishnu laughed and said, "Narada, you are undoubtedly a great devotee of mine, but you are not crazy enough to offer me your own liver. You are a great scholar and your knowledge prevents you from having the craziness of a bhakta. The man who gave you his liver is my true devotee, a true bhakta who cares not for his own life. He only had to hear from you that I was in pain. He did not ask any questions, he did not ask you your identity, he simply acted with the pure devotion of divine love. He is also the same beggar who gave the three sons to the merchant and his wife. I am bound by the chains of such pure love, and must act as one with such bhaktas. Their promises become my promises."

As Narada watched, Vishnu took on the countenance of the beggar and spoke again. "Knowledge and austerity purify the mind, but only the craziness of a bhakta can connect one to me. I and my bhakta are one." And Vishnu ascended to Vaikuntha, leaving Narada in the deepest state of meditation he had ever known.

The princess held a garland of flowers in her hands

Narada's Infatuation

arada, the wandering sage, once decided to dedicate himself to hard penance in order to bring himself to a new level of enlightenment. He secluded himself in a cave and for several years he entered a state of complete meditation called samadhi. Indra, the lord of the elemental gods, feared that Narada would grow so powerful that he would usurp Indra's place, so he sent Kama, the god of love and sensuality, with two celestial nymphs to distract Narada and bring an end to his samadhi.

Kama found Narada meditating with his eyes closed in the middle of winter. With a wave of his hand Kama created springtime in the cave. Birds of every sort sang gaily around the sage, and flowers burst into bloom. Still Narada did not move from his lotus posture. The air warmed Narada's skin, and honeysuckle vines climbed up his body and wafted

They fell to the ground, trembling

perfume in his nostrils. Still he did not react.

Kama told the celestial nymphs to dance. They danced their most beguiling dance in front of Narada, swaying their bodies in ecstasy. They sang songs of pure liquid delight. But Narada never flinched, and Kama stopped his tricks. At that moment Narada opened his eyes, and divine radiance shot out of them and enveloped Kama and the nymphs. They fell to the ground, trembling. Kama prostrated himself in front of Narada and said, "I apologize for my offense, O great one. Please forgive me."

Narada excused Kama with a noble gesture and returned to his Samadhi. Kama and the nymphs left, but Narada found it impossible to return to the deep level of meditation he had achieved. His mind hummed with the joy of his triumph over the god of love. He knew he would not calm down until he let someone know, so he decided to go tell Brahma, the Creator, who was also Narada's father, for

Brahma and Savitri were happy to see Narada

Narada had been born from his mind.

Brahma and his wife Savitri were happy to see Narada, who proceeded to narrate his victory over Kama in minute detail. Brahma blessed him to have even more self-control in the future and asked if Narada would stay with him for a time.

"Thank you, father," said Narada, "but I must go to Mount Kailash to visit Lord Shiva and tell him of my victory. He also loves me and will enjoy hearing the tale."

"Very well," said Brahma. "But I warn you, my son. Do not go tell Vishnu of your success. Your triumph has made you quite fond of yourself, and Vishnu eats egotism."

Narada promised that he would not tell Vishnu and took his leave. Soon he reached Mount Kailash, where he was warmly welcomed by Shiva and Shakti. A garland of flowers was placed around his neck by Nandi, Shiva's faithful servant. "So, Narada," said Shiva, "why have you not visited my kingdom for so many years?"

Narada told Shiva of his penance and his victory over Kama. Shiva congratulated him and asked if he had told his heavenly father yet.

"Yes," said Narada, "he was the first that I told."

"And what did he say?"

"He was pleased to hear the news, but he advised me

Vishnu was as always relaxing on the coiled body of Shesha

not to tell Vishnu."

"I will give you the same advice. It is all right to tell your father and me about your triumph, because we appreciate such things. Vishnu, however, is the preserver of the universe, and he seeks to balance all victories with defeats."

"Thank you for your concern," said Narada, "but Vishnu also loves me, and knows that I am his ardent devotee. He would want to know of my deeds."

"If you are determined to tell him, I will not stop you. But please be humble in the telling."

"Of course," said Narada, and he left Mount Kailash. Soon he reached Vaikuntha and Lord Vishnu, who as always was relaxing on the coiled body of his companion Shesha, the thousand-headed snake. Narada began his tale, careful to be humble and to focus on the depth of his samadhi.

As he listened a smile crossed Lord Vishnu's face. When

Narada told how spring had bloomed around him and he hadn't even noticed, Vishnu laughed and clapped his hands together and said, "Oh, Narada, you are so clever!"

"Well," said Narada, "I admit it was a remarkable feat. But listen to what happened next! Celestial nymphs danced for me, yet I never wavered."

"Truly there is no other mortal like you."

"I believe you are correct. In the end, I filled my body with divine radiance, and Kama himself trembled at my feet!"

Vishnu laughed even harder. "What a delightful tale! Indeed, your story makes me think that you have come to me at the perfect time. I need to send someone to the king of Srinagar to help him, and it sounds like you are the one for the job."

"I would be glad to offer my expertise," said Narada. He thought to himself, *Shiva and Brahma were wrong to worry what Vishnu would think of my tale. He understands me perfectly.*

Narada traveled to the kingdom of Srinagar. The king was honored to have the great sage Narada in his courtroom, especially when Narada announced that he was the envoy of Vishnu himself. He gave Narada his own throne and sat down at his feet. "Great sage," he said, "I have a daughter who is ready to be married, but I do not know how to find a suitable husband for her. You are a great scholar and your knowledge of astrology is unparalleled. Also, you are the most famous wanderer in all the world, so if anybody would know of a good husband for her it is you. I would be most grateful if you would look at her horoscope and read her palm."

Narada said that he would be happy to. He was taken to an inner courtyard where his feet were bathed and he was honored with flowers and fruit. The king soon arrived with his wife and his daughter. Narada was stunned by the daughter's beauty, and he felt a twinge of desire for her himself. He read her birth chart and the palm of her left hand. As he did so he grew more and more amazed. Finally he sat back, breathless with excitement, and said, "Your daughter, O king, is fortunate beyond belief. The one she marries is destined to be lord of the three worlds."

The king and his wife clasped hands, overjoyed at the news. Narada, meanwhile, cast his eyes toward the beautiful body of the princess and found to his astonishment that she had every one of the marks that bring good fortune. To the king he said, "You must arrange a swayambara, a reception where the princess can meet all her suitors and choose one. The one she is to marry will be there. The most auspicious time would be the day of the full moon in the coming ascending fortnight."

Arrangements were made. The more time passed, the more Narada became infatuated by the charming princess of Srinagar. Most of all, he wished to become lord of the three worlds. He decided to attend the swayambara himself. But he was not attractive. If he could only borrow the countenance of Lord Vishnu, then surely the princess would choose him.

Narada returned to Vaikuntha. "Everything is going well, my Lord," he said to Vishnu. "But I have fallen in love with the princess. I would like to end my life of asceticism and marry her. But alas, she would never choose one as ugly as me. If you would be so kind as to lend me your countenance for the day of the swayambara, I am sure she will select me."

"I will indeed help you," said Vishnu. "I am your well-wisher and always do what is in your best interests. When the swayambara comes I will change your countenance."

"Thank you so much, my Lord," said Narada excitedly. "I will be forever in your debt."

Narada spent the days before the swayambara daydreaming about his new life. He could not tell which he desired more—the beautiful princess or being lord of the three worlds.

The day of the swayambara finally arrived, and princes came from all the neighboring kingdoms. Word had spread far and wide of the beauty of the princess, and Narada saw that all the most handsome, intelligent, and powerful young men of the land were there. As he approached the entrance to the great courtyard, Narada said, "All right, my Lord, it is time to change my countenance."

Vishnu's voice sounded in his ear. "It is done."

When Narada looked down, he was wearing Vishnu's robes. He reached up and felt Vishnu's crown on his head. He wished he had a mirror, to see how handsome he looked, but there was no time. Narada entered the court-yard and joined the throng of suitors. He noticed the others glancing at him in surprise. They have never seen the likes of me, he thought contentedly to himself.

When everyone had taken their seats the king addressed them, elaborating the qualities of his beautiful daughter. After he had finished the princess entered the courtyard, holding a garland of flowers in her hand. The princes all stood. Whomever she hung the garland on would be her husband.

The princess slowly walked down the central aisle, glanc-ing at each suitor. Narada waited patiently, certain that he was the most attractive candidate. When she neared him the princess stopped and stared into his face. Then she began to smile. Narada smiled and bent down to let her place the garland around his neck.

The princess stepped up to Narada. . . and stepped past him! Narada straightened up to see Vishnu standing radiant beside him. The princess hung her garland around Vishnu and everyone cheered because it only seemed right that one of such beauty should become the consort of the Lord

Preserver.

Narada, however, was furious. He shook his fist in Vishnu's face, saying "You, Vishnu, have betrayed me! You have broken your promises! You said you would help, and then you stole my rightful wife from me! She would have chosen me, were it not for you."

There was a stunned silence, and then the princess began to giggle. Soon her maidservants were giggling, and then the entire congregation was in an uproar, laughing at Narada. This only made the sage more furious. "What is so funny?" he demanded.

"Do you truly believe that the princess would ever choose you?" said a man beside Narada.

"And why not?"

"Please bring this man a mirror," said the king.

Two of the king's men brought a mirror and handed it to Narada. He looked in it, and staring back at him between the robes of Vishnu and the crown was a monkey. Narada gasped in embarassment, and the whole congregation laughed even harder.

Now Narada was truly in a rage. "As I am suffering the pain of losing this maiden now," he said to Vishnu, "so I hope you will have to suffer the pain of separation from your new wife, and this monkey face you have given me will be the only friend you can find. And these two men who enjoyed bringing me this mirror so much will be doomed to live as demons in their next incarnation!"

Lord Vishnu stood quietly next to his new bride with his hands folded in respect. When Narada had finally run out of breath Vishnu said, "Narada, I accept your curse, which I trust will somehow benefit the world in the long run. Please be calm and see that the one I have married is none other than Lakshmi, my eternal counterpart, who was reincarnated as the daughter of the king of Srinagar because of a curse. I felt certain that when you read her birth chart and saw the

Narada looked at his reflection in the mirror

marks on her body you would know this and arrange things accordingly, but apparently your desire clouded your mind. Who, other than me, could be Lord of the three worlds? You above all people should know this, but clearly whatever state of enlightenment you achieved in your victory over Kama has been destroyed by your own self-love. I have not broken a single promise to you. I did change your countenance, and I did exactly what I thought was in your best interests. Even so, I beg your forgiveness."

The words of Vishnu dispelled Narada's pride like the sun clears mist from a lake. Narada's mind became clear and he fell down at the feet of Lord Vishnu, tears falling to the floor. "It is you who must forgive me, my Lord, for cursing the one who has saved me from folly. I will return to my penance, and try to be more successful this time." And Narada stayed on the floor of the courtyard for a long time, feeling the stings of the arrows of Kama, who is not easily defeated.

Other Titles by Harish Johari

The Birth of the Ganga

Illustrated by Harish Johari and Pieter Weltevrede

This book will delight readers young and old alike with its wonderful story and exquisite hand-painted silk illustrations that bring to life the beautiful goddess Ganga and many other saints and gods from Hindu scripture.

ISBN 0-89281-690-2
$25.00 cloth, 96 pages, 9 x 12
47 color plates

These and other Inner Traditions titles are available at many fine bookstores or to order directly from the publisher, please send a check or money order payble to *Inner Traditions* for the total amount, plus $3.50 shipping and handling for the first book and $1.00 for each additional book to:

> Inner Traditions, P.O. Box 388, Rochester, VT 05767
> or call 1-800-246-8648

Visit our web site: www.gotoit.com

The Healing Cuisine
India's Art of Ayurvedic Cooking

Author, artist, and world-renowned scholar of Tantra and Ayurveda, Harish Johari is also an inspired and accomplished cook who shares his culinary wisdom in this treasury of vegetarian cooking based on Ayurvedic principles of healing. Ayurveda places great emphasis on diet and the specific attributes of foods. Following these time-honored principles, Johari explains the healing qualities of foods and spices and indicates which combinations are appropriate for specific conditions of body and mind. Ten years in the making, this beautiful book is filled with recipes that bring the depth of Ayurvedic knowledge to the delightful experience of preparing and sharing sumptuous meals that feed both body and soul.

ISBN 0-89281-382-2 • $16.95 pb

Breath, Mind, and Consciousness

Modern scientists are just beginning to understand what yogis have known for centuries—that the life force animating our bodies is regulated by breath, and that breath energy is controlled by the mind. The science of Swar Yoga—presented in this book for the first time in English—teaches conscious observation and control of breathing patterns to maximize energy and vitality. Harish Johari brings his extensive knowledge of ancient Hindu science to this discussion of breath and the yoga of balanced living, drawing on information from original Sanskrit texts otherwise unavailable in the English language.

ISBN 0-89281-252-4 • $9.95 pb

Tools For Tantra

In this handsome companion volume to *Chakras,* Harish Johari illustrates the ancient yantras, geometric designs which have been used for centuries in India as visual aids to the experience of Tantra. Until his careful research and replication of the yantras, their spiritual applications, forms, and colors were largely lost to the modern world. Johari explains the traditional Hindu practices associated with yantras, including techniques for meditation and visualization, and concludes with a full description of the Tantric ritual.

> *"A true renaissance man, this distinguished North Indian poet, sculptor, and musician holds degrees in philosophy and literature. In this book, he delivers a fine exposition on Tantra. This volume features a bounty of rare yogic lore."*
>
> East West Journal

ISBN 0-89281-055-6 • $18.95 pb
20 full-color plates, 35 line drawings

Sounds of Tantra

Mantra Meditation Techniques from Tools for Tantra

A companion to his book *Tools for Tantra, Sounds of Tantra* provides exact pronunciation of mantras, or words of power. Meditate on the colorful geometric paintings of yantras in the book while listening to the tape, combining visual and auditory elements, or simply listen to the tapes as background for meditation.

ISBN 0-89281-016-5
$15.95 Boxed set of two 60-minute audiocassettes

Chakras

Energy Centers of Transformation

This beautifully illustrated companion volume to *Tools for Tantra* introduces the classical principles of the chakras and shows their practical applications for today. Artist and Tantric scholar Harish Johari illustrates the images of each energy center, providing a focus for meditation, as he correlates each chakra with appropriate mantras, colors, astrological signs, and deities, as well as with personality types and behavioral characteristics.

> *"Johari's text is among the best of Western explications, combining traditional, visionary, and practical views. It is illustrated, detailed, accessible to the neophyte, and notable for its valuable discussions."*
>
> East West Journal

ISBN 0-89281-054-8 • $14.95 pb
9 full-color plates, 12 line drawings

The Healing Power of Gemstones

In Tantra, Ayurveda, and Astrology

Drawing on the ancient Hindu sciences of Tantra, Ayurvedic medicine, and astrology, as well as his own family tradition of gemology, Johari has developed methods for using the power stored in gems to maximize physical and psychological balance and health.

From the formulation of healing gem powders, to the appropriate gems to be worn according to your sun sign and ascendant, this comprehensive work serves as a practical guide to the chemical and subtle nature of gemstones and offers a traditional overview of their applications throughout history.

ISBN 0-89281-608-2 • $14.95 pb

Leela: The Game of Self-Knowledge

The origin of Herman Hesse's *Glass Bead Game* and the precursor to the popular game "chutes and ladders," Leela is the 2,000-year-old Hindu game of life, in which players' progress is directed by the fall of a die. Repeated play will reveal past karmas, concern, and the patterns governing your life. Leela is both entertaining and enlightening, and represents the spiritual journey toward liberation.

> *"Unlocks the knowledge of the Vedas, Shrutis, Smiritis and Puranas. A seriously fun way to discover self."*
>
> The Book Reader

ISBN 0-89281-419-5
$24.95 Boxed set, book, game board, and die

Numerology

With Tantra, Ayurveda, and Astrology

For the first time, a system of numerology has been developed that encompasses the ancient Hindu sciences of Tantra, Ayurveda, and Astrology. Harish Johari explains how to determine your psychic, name, and destiny numbers; how they relate to each of the nine planets; and what they reveal about your personality, temperament, intelligence, talents, sexuality, spirituality, finances, travel, and health. Recommendations are given regarding strong and weak periods of day or year, favorable colors and precious stones to be worn, and meditations and mantras to be practiced for health and prosperity.

ISBN 0-89281-258-3 • $12.95 pb

Chants to the Sun and Moon
Japa for Energizing the Planets Within
Japa—the repetition of a mantra—is an age-old Hindu technique for drawing down a planet's positive energy. On this recording, Harish Johari chants the preferred number of repetitions of the mantras traditionally associated with the sun and moon. During meditation, the practitioner not only hears the mantras intoned by an expert, but is freed from the distraction of counting.
ISBN 0-89281-563-9
$9.95 one 60-minute audiocassette

Sounds Of The Chakras
A companion to *Chakras: Energy Centers of Transformation,* this audiocassette provides the accurate sounds for meditation on each of the chakras. Johari goes through the entire intonation cycle that is to be practiced with chakra meditation in a way that the student can follow with ease.
ISBN 0-89281-307-5
$9.95 one 60-minute audiocassette

Attunements for Dawn And Dusk
Drawing upon ancient Indian ragas, or musical compositions, Harish Johari creates meditation music especially for the early morning and evening hours, inspired by the sounds of nature, which vary depending upon the hour of the day. Flute for Dawn, Tambura for Morning Meditation, and Flute and Bird for Dusk are just a few of the selections included.
ISBN 0-89281-370-9
$15.95 Boxed set of two 60-minute audiocassettes